The Rising of The Elements

Curtis Smith

Copyright © 2016 Curtis Smith

All rights reserved.

ISBN: 150071397X
ISBN-13: 978-1500713973

FOR THE FUTURE

CONTENTS

	Acknowledgments	i
1	Holograms	1
2	Isaac's Choice	13
3	Instigate The Elements	36
4	Reality of The Elements	59
5	The Formulation	79
6	The Triad of Canorum	114
7	The Bellators and The Boy	178
8	Elementarium	202
9	The Battle of The Elements	237
	Epilogue	267

ACKNOWLEDGMENTS

I'd like to thank, of course, my family for their utmost support from the offset and allowing me the time and space to write.

I'd like to thank many of my close and distant friends, some I do not even speak to nowadays, for influencing and inspiring me to the greatest extent. Perhaps unbeknownst to them, because we are still so young, they've been proving how being different can be a true advantage in life, which has been a huge source of self-development and inspiration. Specifically, Anand, Giles, Ellen, Jacob, Giorgia, Hannah, Harriet, Leanne, Alex, Jordan, Hollie, Katie, Katherine, Izzy, Beth, Emma, Mina, Emily, James, Chris, Steve, Joe, Arafath, Khuda, Gemma and Matt.

I'd like to thank Alice, Sophia, David, Oli and Dan for evoking my stark curiosity and admiration for the world and society. Thank you for showing me that anybody can be important to you, no matter where they come from.

Without any person who has ever been in my life this story wouldn't be what it is.

Embracing fear and fighting adversity with hope, unity and coexistence.

Chapter One: Holograms

"Don't be afraid" Mother whispers to me, as I contemplate the elements. Buildings in my town campaign for each element, with holograms above them. Fire, Water, Earth and Air.

A ticking noise commences. A gust of wind throwing me back to the ground, three stories below where I stood. Mother comes running down the stairs while I struggle to stand. She reaches her hand out to me as I reach towards her.

She lifts me up and pats my back, fortunately I landed

on a soft area of grass so I'm not heavily injured, which is a disappointment to say the least. It would get me out of fighting the elements.

Mother chose Fire and survived with third degree burns plastered on her arm, a heavy marking of the Fire symbol was left, an imprint of her helpless fight against a prosthetic creation.

"We need to get you signed on"

"Signed on?" I question.

"Don't tell me you've forgotten about signing on? You haven't decided, have you?" Mother ferociously screams at me.

If I choose Fire, it's an unwritten fundamental obligation to be burnt to the core until you psychologically shatter. People die because of Fire years after the fight. It sticks with them. It squats in their bodies until they're practically empty and it takes over, destroying them. Mother guesses she has a couple of years to go, one at the least. I don't *mean* destroyed metaphorically, people physically combust because of the tormenting infectious flames that writhe through their bodies. Water is just as ghastly, it's said to feel like drowning, overtaking your character and emotionally turning you into something undead, and if you manage to survive? The Water levels in your body rise to the point where you begin to seep Water, every cell in your body is ravaged.

This only happens if you let the elements control you, if you're strong enough then you won't experience the trauma, that is *if* you defeat the element.

You see, the elements aren't a way of maintaining the fittest; it's a complementary way of decreasing the population. It's a way of making the bourgeoisie even more elite, because they don't *have* to fight.

"Have you considered Earth and Air?" Mother asks me.

"No. Not really."

"Isaac, I can't lose another child, not after your Sister."

Amara, she chose Earth.

Mother turns quiet; she faces away from me, as if I disgust her. I turn back, and see two young women. The two recognise me, yet look at me in sorrow. I redden as I realise they must have witnessed my fall. One is called Sophia Bell, she's chirpy and energetic, the opposite to the other girl, Alice Levingston. Alice is intelligent and kind-hearted. They wave, knowing that in a week I'll undoubtedly be dead. Sophia contested Air and won. She became an instant celebrity after defeating the element after only ten seconds, most dying after seven. Alice chose Fire, foolishly. She defeated the element after two minutes, and, likewise, went on to become a local celebrity for her theatrical skills, performing for adolescents in which she includes concealed messages about each element. The two girls laugh as children as young as eight ask for a picture with them, Sophia seems to accept her newfound fame, however Alice seems more modest, gasping as she is recognised. I notice a scar on Sophia's left arm. This scar shows the symbol of the Air element, like the one shown on the hologram, yet I fail to understand how this came to be. Surely Air cannot wound you. A child grabs her arm and she yells. The child darts away in sheer terror as Sophia leans against the wall, the scar beginning to throb, radiating a grey light. Alice comforts the remaining children, content to see that they are witnessing the effect of Air. I rush over to help the suffering girl; she tells me to leave and begins to scream. Sophia fought the element years ago and she's still struggling, I don't know if I can do it. I don't know if I can survive. Alice, very much out of character, reassures the children that Sophia is fine; however, we both can see that Sophia is in agony so we tell the children to leave. Sophia drops to the floor and quickly loses her breath; Alice kneels by her side and holds her hand. I look to Mother, who's a doctor, but she stands there helplessly. Perhaps medicine cannot overpower the elements.

"Breathe. Remember, Sophia. One… two… three." Alice says in sheer desperation.

Sophia continues to struggle breathing, resting her head on Alice's knee, looking at me and shedding a tear. This isn't a tear of pain; it's more like a tear of sympathy. She whispers her regrets, her voice sounding lifeless and inane. Her grey eyes become still, her arms falling to the ground, Alice closes the lifeless body's eyes as Mother grabs my arm and drags me away.

"We're going home".

"But Mother, you're a doctor, help her."

I turn to Sophia and Alice; Alice is snivelling over the body of Sophia. A troop of subordinates, the assistants to Deatra, the local life monitor, rush out of the medical centre and surround Sophia. Alice begins to wail; I turn away to see what seems to be the whole community witnessing this ordeal. They are hiding their faces, in what is possibly a sign of respect. To my left I see the Elemental Dome, a hologram of the Domain Balls, which contain the elements, is shown in the sky. To my right, I see continuous rows of houses, outside each home a subordinate stands facing the door. Families peer through the windows, as if they're trapped. A flame triggers behind me, where Sophia's body lays lifeless. Mother opens the door to my home, and throws me onto the settee.

I'm confused, looking around the home as a subordinate walks up to the front and simply stands. I give the subordinate a fleeting look, as if to tell him to leave. He draws a gun as I close the curtains.

"Mother, what's going on?" I enquire frantically.

Mother rushes into the kitchen, and breathes heavily. She rests against the counter. I walk towards her, but she shouts and tells me to stay away. She begins to tremble; I scuttle backwards into the hall. The subordinate outside my home begins to walk closer to the front door. Mother lowers to the floor, the marking of the Fire symbol beginning to smoulder, causing agony. Her rouge eyes begin to turn insipid. Her body is laid out across the cold floor; her breathing begins to quiet and becomes gradual. Deatra's subordinates race into the home and push me aside.

"What is this woman's name? What relation is she to you?" A man asks.

I fail to answer, because I am so distracted by his character. His hair is a gradient of grey to red, his eyebrows are a sharp red, and his eyes a subdued grey. He is familiar, but how could I recognise a stranger? As I selfishly study the peculiar character even more, while Mother is dying, the man grows more recognisable. He stands up, and comes towards me. The man smacks me.

"What is her name? Who is she?"

Startled, I reply "My Mother. Eliza Williams."

The man steps back, he looks shaken, suddenly unnerved. He asks his fellow subordinates to deal with 'the matter', and looks to me. He smiles, hiding his curious sorrow. He begins to well up.

"You're Isaac?" He asks. "Isaac Williams?"

"What does it matter to you?" I snap.

The subordinates carry Mothers body away, through the front door and into a crystal white box. The box makes a clicking sound, and flies up into the air. Mother, she's gone. I don't know how to feel. I walk up the stairs and through the door to my bedroom. Pressing a button on the wall, which activates a menu from the side of my bed. Browsing through, I find an option named 'solemnity'. I press the activation button, and the lights in my bedroom turn off, the curtains shut automatically and a holographic image of a forest is projected onto my wall. I lean against the wall, and slowly sink to the ground. For once, despite the sadness, I feel content. The forest being projected against my wall makes me feel isolated, which I find is best for a situation like this. Orchestral music begins playing through the speakers in my walls; it's not as fitting as I had hoped. I'm not really a huge fan of orchestral music, it's not lively. But, considering what just occurred, I'd rather not listen to anything lively. Everything in my bedroom turns black; leaving my living body bundled against a holographic forest. I struggle to hold back the tears as I wail for Mother, a photograph of her lies on my shelf, amongst this photograph is a framed picture of my Father, who has also passed, and Amara. I am alone, alone in this world of survival and competition.

The peculiar subordinate from before comes into my bedroom, hidden in the darkness. The man sets the lighting to 'vivid', and I can see him fully. He wears a name badge; I quickly identify him as Claude Bellator.

"I've been instructed to stay with you until the day you fight your element, it's just a week." He says, attempting to be caring, yet failing miserably.

"Okay." I bluntly respond.

He sits beside me, against a plain white wall, the holographic forest having been turned off by his incompetence. He tries to comfort me, yet I move further away like a child. He hesitates, and then stands up. He catches the attention of the photograph of Mother and sighs. He even looks fairly similar in appearance to the woman in the picture. I think nothing of it and rest on my bed, as I lie down I feel the bed surround me. I close my eyes and leave everything behind. I hear Claude shut my bedroom door.

I open my eyes, and see Mother lying on a white slab, floating in a room with all four walls painted black. I hastily stand up and move towards her, attempting to hold her but my hand going straight through her body, ripples form and a blue light stutters around her. Her eyes open, Mother is pale, and she doesn't look how she did before. Her mouth opens, as if she's trying to say something.

"Trust yourself"

Suddenly, her body disappears. The floor beneath me fades away, and I fall onto the floor below. In this room, there are three doors. One opens and Amara walks in, ghostlike. The second and third doors open to reveal Mother and my Father. They walk towards me, reaching out for me. Father takes me and throws me against the wall, Mother and Amara laugh as I struggle.

"Isaac, don't be such a child. You're supposed to be strong, like a man!" Father says.

The three of them stand next to each other, and reach out for me once again. Their hands close onto my neck.

I scream and their spirits evaporate, I hear their strident cries as my eyes close.

THE RISING OF THE ELEMENTS

I am surrounded with silence, and I feel as if I am floating. The silence overwhelms me and I fall asleep once more.

Chapter Two: Isaac's Choice

It's been six days since Mother passed. The Fire element got into her blood and she died on the spot. No illness, just death. *Just life*. Claude is still here, obviously. I'm still trying to decipher the mystery that is Claude Bellator. I've come to the conclusion that some mysteries should remain unsolved.

Claude has quickly become comfortable in *my* house, he tends to walk around and sing obnoxiously to ancient pop songs about the derrière, much to my disapproval. It does cheer me up though; it gives me comfort to know that somebody could be happy enough to sing disgustingly around a stranger like myself. I presume I'm jovial, despite Mother no longer being here. It's nice to be heard, when I'm not often given the opportunity to be listened to.

I walk into the kitchen only to find Claude sitting at the table.

"Are you ready? For tomorrow?" He asks with a poor attempt of sensitivity.

The element fight is tomorrow. I'm hardly looking forward to it. I handed in my confirmation slip yesterday; I can't help but think that it all seems a bit silly that I have to confirm my impending doom on a formal piece of paper.

"So, what element did you choose?" Claude questions me.

I shake my head, implying to him that I failed to do so. He looks awfully disappointed. Why should he care? He's a subordinate. I am of no importance to the fool anyway. Claude stands up and leaves the room; he bolts up the stairs and sits at the top.

"What's wrong with you?" I shout "It's not like they'll put all four elements against me!"

Claude puts his hand against the back of his neck and smiles, as if he's about to tell me something eternally disappointing.

"Isaac, remember that mostly everyone has a characteristic based on their element. Your Mother had rouge eyes and the Fire marking, Sophia had grey highlights in her hair. So why is it that I have grey and red hair?" He asks, rhetorically. "I didn't choose my element, so I was given Air and Fire. I hardly made it out alive."

"Two elements aren't that bad, Claude." I tell the worried man.

"My Sister, Ange, she didn't choose as well. There were four others battling on the same day as her, two chose Air, one chose Fire, and the last chose Water. That left Ange, and everybody else, thinking she would fight Earth. She entered the Elemental Dome Ring, and as she turned around to see the Domain Balls, she saw four. After being singed, swept around and almost drowning, Earth claimed her with a branch through her heart." Claude begins to cry. "Do you understand? They can give you one element, but they can also give you more."

Suddenly, Claude scuttles out of the house, pushing me aside whilst doing so. I glance outside to see him moving towards the Elemental Dome, he begins to disappear in the fog. I startle as I realise what I'd just seen. Why is there fog in June? I move towards the haze, only to hear miniscule shrill cries. The mist races around me, surrounding me as I struggle to move back into my house. I begin to deafen from the high-pitched noise, collapsing onto the ground and attempting to scramble towards the door. A gunshot is fired, and the mist rises up into the atmosphere and all is transparent again. I run to the Council Building in an attempt to discover what the abnormal mist was. Deatra and her team of subordinates swagger through the quarter, the subordinates carrying their heads in shame, facing the ground while pompous Deatra holds her head up high. Deatra wears a white suit, with her black hair flowing down to her waist, with a purple braid running through the middle parting. She glares at me, and I begin to feel disconcerted, as if she's inferring that I am beneath her, that she is at the highest point of the hierarchy. Deatra likes to think of herself as a queen. I personally feel that she's too much of a narcissistic tyrant to be royal, although that hasn't stopped them before. Deatra approaches me, and her subordinates seem to be in a trance, either a trance or they are too afraid to disobey her.

"I presume you *are* Isaac Williams?" She asks, compelling me to look at her in repugnance. "We are truly sorry for the loss of your Mother, Eliza Williams. She was an asset to the community."

I can detect sarcasm here, as Deatra seems to unwillingly smile after every word she spits out of her vile mouth.

"However, I must inform you that the Fire element infected her blood and killed her a week before her ultimate death." Deatra declares.

"How can that be? I spoke to her in the morning." I

retaliate.

"Indeed you did, Eliza Williams was indeed moving for a week after her death. However, I am to explain for that. We tested on her body for a week succeeding her death; this meant that we needed her to act habitually. The best way of doing so was through me. Your Mother did have a conscience for that last week, however, it wasn't hers. *I* was managing her. Oh, I'm sorry for the inconvenience; it is simply that your Mother was worthless during the experiment, a bit boring, so I let her drop dead in front of you." Deatra smiles as she says this, and intentionally has a moment of laughter.

As I hear this, anger begins to spread through my veins violently. I feel the compulsion to tear Deatra apart limb by limb, and feed her to a gluttonous goat, for Deatra is worthless, *not* my Mother. The sheer persecution coming from Deatra infuriates me, I look up to her and push her. Deatra falls to the ground as I shout at her, screaming and kicking.

Deatra stands and strikes me, as I feel this I kick her

backwards.

"You're supposed to be the life monitor, you foul woman." I announce.

Deatra holds me by the neck, and lifts me up. Her strength surprises me; you would not expect this from a vain dictator. I begin to lose my breath, and my sight begins to obscure. She claws into my neck, and I gasp for any sign of air. I can feel my legs become dead, the feeling spreads through the rest of my body. I look at the subordinates, and see a woman with burgundy eyes facing down; the woman has red tips in her hair.

"You" I say, attempting to get her attention.

The woman looks up, and Deatra turns her head in astonishment. Deatra throws me down to the ground, and I'm unable to move. I look at the woman closer, and search for her name badge as she increasingly becomes more recognisable. Deatra attempts to obscure the name badge, yet I'm able to quickly make it out.

THE RISING OF THE ELEMENTS

Eliza Williams

Deatra comes towards me with a tranquiliser, and puts me to sleep. As this happens, I hear a gunshot, followed by the cries of Mother and the laughter of Deatra. I fall into a deep sleep, and find myself in a state of dreaming. I am in the same dark room as before, a figure is sat in the corner. The four elemental symbols appear on each wall, emitting a light of their colour. I move towards the figure; the symbols begin to fade as I reach out for her. A light is projected from my hand as I wave over her; I discover that the figure is Mother. This time I'm able to touch her, I turn her around and she wilts onto the floor. Her hair is covering her face, and she is covered by a black sheet. As I attempt to move the hair from her face, the floor underneath me collapses and I, again, fall into the room below. The body follows me and rolls out from under the sheet, to my surprise Deatra lies where Mother should be. She stands and brings out a knife, her eyes glazed and her lipstick smeared. She stands in the corner opposite me, and two doubles appear in the two remaining corners. The three Deatra's come towards me, wielding the same knife, and raise their hands simultaneously. Claude materialises behind them, and wounds the authentic Deatra, with the two copies merging into her. Deatra falls to the ground and grabs Claude, he falls to the ground and the two begin to fight. A jewelled crown appears on Deatra's head, and begins to trickle with blood. Deatra screams as her face becomes blood stained, and covers her wound quickly. Claude puts his arm around her throat and threatens to kill her. I tell him to stop but they cannot hear me. Deatra screams as Claude emits fire from his right hand, and burns her neck. A howling wind can be heard as I shout for Claude to stop. He looks at me; he can hear me. Deatra is sprawled on the floor; I notice that she has no characteristics that define her element, just hints of the colour purple. Claude produces wind from his left hand and throws me against the wall, and I am unable to move because of its strength. Deatra's crown liquefies altogether, leaving a tarn of blood on the floor. The blood begins to glimmer, and turns black.

"What have you done with Eliza?" Claude asks Deatra.

"Why? Was she of any importance to you?" Deatra counteracts.

"You know she was important, Deatra."

"She was a pathetic excuse for a human being, it's 2057." Deatra cackles. "Sensitivity will get you nowhere, she was dying anyway."

As Deatra says this, she pulls out a teleportation device and frantically presses it. Claude pulls down the wall of wind he was using to hold against me, and I leap onto Deatra just as she teleports. I find myself travelling through a threshold where the four colours of the elements flash before my eyes. I cling onto Deatra for dear life, and she attempts to kick me off. I can hear Claude shouting my name in the distance; I get the feeling that I haven't done the right thing. Deatra unreasonably stings my hand with a solution that turns my hands numb, and I begin to lose my grip. Deatra disappears as I begin to fall upwards into a blinding light; Claude's shouting becoming more distant. I fall onto a floor that holds an image of the Great British flag; I stand up to see a noble door in front of me, towering over my insignificant body. I turn the handle, and peer inside the room. Paintings of Deatra hang on a wall; the paintings have graffiti over them, with the words 'save us' written in blood appearing on each one. A red carpet leads to a door adjacent to me, I step on the carpet and I drop through the floor to a new room. This new room features holograms of people; curiously I stroll through hoping to find somebody I recognise. Each person has a label, with names varying from Philip King to Aurelia Swan, as I progress through each hologram; I come across one that I recognise. However, there doesn't seem to be a label identifying who she is.

"I know you." I whisper, formulating a label which appears in my hand.

Amara Williams

My Sister, why is her hologram here? Each hologram in the room turns into Amara. I run for the door as the holograms become real.

"Run." Amara says, simultaneously.

Each copy of Amara begins to laugh uncontrollably; they surround me as I begin to shout for them to stop. Each Amara breaks down and curls up into a ball on the floor, they begin to disintegrate with only one remaining. I approach Amara and attempt to comfort her, as I touch her face Amara's skin starts to melt, showing a metal frame underneath, yet still the sound of her tears encompasses me. The metal frame dissembles and turns into a black liquid that moulds to form a black figure, the mould is of me. Every move I make is paralleled by the figure, yet cat-like eyes form on it. The eyes turn red, and the figure slowly morphs into Mother, she takes my hand and pulls me to the ground. I look above to see a square, dislodged from the rest of the ceiling. Escape. In the far corner of the room I see a ball of fire forming, it jets towards me as I lean against the floor in desperation. The figure flies back and hits the wall, it begins to fade away. The room rotates, the ceiling is now the floor. I open up the displaced square, and see

Claude buckled to a chair, Deatra strolls past him and pushes him over. Claude looks up and notices me looking in from the ceiling, he gives me an imperative glance so I close the square and stand up.

The room has changed; I look around to find trees looming over me. There are no walls, simply an eternal rainforest. Parakeets fly over me, and land on a cage that entraps a golden eagle. A noise occurs behind me; I ask if anybody's there only to get no response. I turn back to see the parakeets have flown away, and the eagle begins to unnerve inside the cage. Five keys appear on five different trees; I gather them all and attempt to open the cage to free the golden eagle. The cage fails to open. I notice that each key can be taken apart in five segments; I scramble the segments apart on the dirt and choose five unsystematically. I piece together the segments and after a few attempts they eventually fuse together, I place the key into the lock and the cage opens. I carry the eagle with my hand, and attempt to let it fly. The eagle lifts upwards and flies, however it becomes motionless and drops to the ground. I pick the eagle up to discover it has become a statue. The noise occurs again; I turn back to find two lions coming towards me. The lions have the four element symbols engraved on their backs, they snarl and tear towards me. I begin to run from them. They grow closer and closer, I fall to the ground, and the lions run straight through me as if I'm an apparition. The lions continue to sprint through the wilderness, and apes gather in the trees above me. Blood drips onto my shoulder from above. They begin to shriek, racing down the trees to surround my body. The apes morph into Sophia Bell, the girl that died on the day of Mothers passing. Alice Levingston appears behind her, appearing spent. Sophia is lifeless, apart from slowly swaying forwards and backwards. The motion speeds up to an unimaginable pace until Sophia drops to the ground, Alice kneels beside her, kissing her forehead. I'm able to hear the cries of apes coming from the trees, yet I'm no longer able to see them. The sky begins to darken and red stars appear in the sky. Both Sophia and Alice stand, expressionless and unresponsive. The two begin to smile, tilting their heads to the side as they do so. Their eyes are focused on me; they raise their hands as if to signal something. Sophia conjures a wind from her hand, keeping me afloat. Sophia screams uncontrollably.

"You could have helped us, Isaac." Alice remarks. "You could have saved her."

Alice blasts a ball of fire from her hand towards me, I jump backwards only to be brought forwards by Sophia's element. I plead for them to stop.

"What's happening?" I ask, stupidly.

Sophia brings me back down, however whilst I'm floating to the ground an ape-like creature hurdles onto me and begins to gnaw at my shoulder. Alice propels flames towards the ape and it drops to the rainforest floor. The ape transforms into Deatra. Sophia begins to panic as Deatra walks towards her.

"You're supposed to be dead."

Deatra begins to glitch, and blue lights sizzle around the forest. Sophia and Alice step back, while Deatra cuts out. It appears that she is being hacked of some kind; a figure appears in the place where Deatra once stood.

"Isaac, I'm Ange Bellator. Your body is in the Dormiton Building, with Deatra and her subordinates. Look, Sophia and Alice attacked you because they're being controlled by her, we hacked into the system and managed to send the real Alice and Sophia into your dream to protect you, but Deatra got to them too. Your Mother is in the Dormiton Building with you. Claude is here in the Reformation Building, with Sophia, Alice and I. You'll be safe Isaac." She says, and dematerialises.

Ange Bellator? Claude's Sister, she died. At least, that's what Claude told me. Unless he was lying. I turn around and see that Sophia and Alice have disappeared, how is Sophia alive? I have so many unanswered questions. If this is a dream, how do I wake? Ange reappears.

"Isaac, tomorrow you fight the elements. Do *not* win. You have to die. Right now, you need to be in pain to wake up. I've materialised a blade for you, it's by the tree next to you. Deatra's trapped in the threshold, so when you awaken… just *run*, the subordinates are in a trance. Isaac, it's important you listen to me, don't try and save your Mother; just don't. We'll meet you at the Elemental Dome." Again, she dissipates.

I need to die? The cheek of it! I begin to think about how Ange looked, she was strikingly similar to Claude, and had vibrant green eyes and an array of colours in her hair. I stop myself from distraction by pinching myself. I look to the tree to the left of me; a blade is perched on a branch, although I cannot reach it. I collect some fallen branches and pile them on top of each other, it doesn't look safe however I stand on the structure anyway. As I reach for the blade, the branches collapse and my head hits the ground, the blade flies towards me and impales my forehead. I let out a scream of pain, and everything turns dark.

I awaken in a bitter room, everything seems to be white. I'm enclosed in a glass box and lights are shone over me. I try to escape, but the box is locked. A keypad is positioned by my hand; I attempt various codes with no luck. On each wall there is a number, accompanied by an element symbol.

THE RISING OF THE ELEMENTS

Air: 71

Earth: 39

Fire: 02

Water: 48

I type in 71390248 into the keypad, and the glass above me contracts. I lift myself up and out of the box; I walk over to a subordinate and wave my hand in front of him. I am unnoticed. Mother lies in a glass box, marked with the symbol of the fire element. I remember what was said to me. *Run.* I run out the room into a corridor. The corridor seems eternal; as whichever way I go it reappears. I re-enter the room in which I awoke, there is a safe that is marked with 'reverse'. I enter the code I used to escape the box, only to be rejected. Reverse. I enter the code in reverse, 84209317, and the safe opens. There doesn't seem to be much security in this building. Inside the safe are four teleportation devices, I strap one onto my hand and type in 'Elemental Dome', a yellow light appears around me and consumes me. I reappear in the threshold, as I glide through I see images of

Deatra held in a cage. Deatra begins to move in each picture, I realise that this is how they trapped her, she's trapped in the pictures. I approach the end of the threshold, and I appear at the Elemental Dome. The area is clear, inert, yet daunting.

I walk past the main entrance, and into the door behind the building, thinking it would keep me unseen. I creep past the security office, and a man walks out of the room.

Hesitation.

"Isaac Williams?" The burly man asks. "You're early, we were expecting you tomorro'."

"I'm sorry, what for?" I reply, confused.

"For your fight with the elements, of course. Why, what are you 'ere for?" He guides me to the main entrance and tells me to wait until I'm assigned a room for the night.

Sophia and Alice come out of a room, followed by Claude and Ange.

"Where have you been?" Alice asks. "You were supposed to meet us outside the main entrance ten minutes ago!"

"I took the back entrance, I thought it would be better." I answer.

Alice looks furious.

"Cooler." I say under my breath.

Ange Bellator steps forward, she shakes my hand and smiles. On her neck, she has the four element colours tattooed, in a watercolour style. Of course, Ange fought each element. She has a scar that spirals down her arm, and a burn at the ending of the scar.

"How did you survive?" I question.

"Isaac, I can't tell you. You'll find out. All you need to do is, and I say this *with* utmost respect, you need to die." She replies.

"Won't that be obvious?" I ask. "If I just let the elements kill me? Won't they be doubtful?"

"Put up a fight. Try and survive. We'll be there,

Claude and I."

"Claude said you were gone. I still don't understand." I begin to grow confused.

"Isaac, I've already told you. It's confidential."

Ange moves towards Claude and whispers something; I'm unable to make out what she said. The two then walk away, leaving me with Sophia and Alice. They sit beside me, there is an unnerving silence. I start to become exceptionally self-conscious, the two look at me as I fidget. I stand up and begin to pace the room, feeling apprehensive from the silence. I attempt to make conversation, asking how they are and how their family are, with no success. Sophia begins to laugh at me; but Alice tells her to stop and smacks her knee. A cleaner walks into the main entrance with a defective trolley, the noise is unbearable, yet makes the situation much more comfortable. The cleaner looks at me as I stand in the middle of the room, she stares at me as if I'm a mutant, her eyebrows rise in disgust and she embarrassingly smiles at Sophia and Alice, attempting to make as little eye contact as possible. I move back to where the two are sat, and the cleaner moves on while whistling an upbeat tune. As I perch to sit down, I miss the chair and fall promptly onto the floor. The cleaner perks her head around the corner and begins to howl with laughter hysterically, Sophia bursts out laughing as I begin to grow red from embarrassment. Alice begins to laugh as she helps me up, her hand slipping as I fall back down. Could this day be any worse? I feel as if this is the worst part of the day; forget being attacked by Deatra or lions, falling over in front of people will always be a disconcerting misery. As I frantically stand up, I can still hear the cleaner's laughter in the far distance, how pleasant. Sophia stops laughing, but she develops a smirk that suggests she still finds my accident hilarious. I stand up, feeling on edge. *Please don't fall again.* I move towards the chair and my foot hits the chair leg, I falter onto the chair. Sophia, Alice and I begin to laugh; we look up and see a man dressed formally.

"Isaac Williams, we're ready for you now."

The merriment stops, my hands beginning to tremble.

THE RISING OF THE ELEMENTS

I stand up; Sophia and Alice smile and raise their hands to wave me off. I walk past the cleaner but she no longer laughs at me; she holds her head down in sympathy.

A door unbolts in front of me; the man wishes me good fortune and guides me into the room. He leaves me in the midpoint, the door slams behind me. I stand, staring at my reflection, paralleled by four walls glazed with mirrors. The door behind me in which I walked through has disappeared, enclosing me in a wall covered in my reflection. I sit on the floor, anticipating sunrise.

Chapter Three: Instigate the Elements

I've been in the mirrored room for what I predict is a few hours, for that reason suggesting it's the day of the fight. A mirror covers every fragment of the room, including the ceiling and floor. I've grown sick of my reflection, acting like I hate the individual who taunts me in reverse, yet the individual copies every action I do. A crack has formed on the mirror to the left of me, but I daren't attempt to interfere with it in fear of punishment, in apprehension of Deatra.

Yet, temptation overwhelms me and I move towards the fracture, I peer through a small hole to find a girl on the other side in a room exactly like mine. She wears a striped top that reflects profoundly in the mirrored room. I take out a stone I carry for luck in my trouser pocket; I attempt to chisel at the crack, causing grit to fall onto my lap. The girl looks around in an attempt to locate the noise. The hole begins to grow larger, and the girl begins to notice my appearance forming through the wall of reflection. I smile, and throw the stone through the wall in order to regain her attention, as it is lost due to her own consideration of madness. The auspicious stone hits her on the shoulder, and she lets out a frustrated sound. I quickly apologise, and she comes over to the crack in the wall.

"How did you manage to chisel through? These mirrors are too strong to be chiselled through." She asks, her voice being tender yet assertive.

"Just a lucky stone. Actually, could I have that back? It's kind of lucky. I said that already. Sorry." I reply, as she pokes the stone through the small hole. "Thank you; I'm Isaac by the way."

"Jenna, Jenna Sutherland *by the way*." She counteracts mockingly. "What's your element? I'm an Air."

"I haven't chosen." As I say this, Jenna looks at me in disgust. "What's the matter?"

"You're one of *those* people? The people that think they're too *cool* to decide on an element?"

"Cool? I just don't see why it matters." I reply. "We live in a society where only the strongest and the richest survive, I'm not strong. I'm not rich. I'd rather be destroyed by an element than attempt to fight it and harm my family's reputation."

"You're scared of harming your family's reputation? What are you, noble?" She vivaciously retorts.

"Just proud, that's all."

"So you dying wouldn't hurt your family's reputation?"

"My Sister did, she died, but they were proud because she had an element chosen. My Father's dead, and my Mother's not around anymore, I guess." I reply..

Jenna shakes her head, suggesting she doesn't know what I mean.

I notice a change in the floor beneath her, it transforms into a tiled pattern consisting of all four colours. A black square appears in the far corner, words flash through a hologram.

'PLEASE STAND HERE'

The crack closes up, insinuating that those in control are aware of my interaction with Jenna. The mirrors in my room become screens which allow me to watch Jenna's battle.

"Jenna Sutherland, the daughter of Aurelia Swan and Henry Sutherland, born on the 20th of June 2039." An official announces. I recognise the name Aurelia Swan from yesterday.

Jenna walks into the Elemental Dome Ring, and sees a Domain Ball floating in front of her. I look over to the screen adjacent to me to see her family seated above her. Aurelia Swan appears to be a Water element, implied by her stark blue eyes which catch my attention from afar, Henry Sutherland appears to be an Air, I conclude by his grey hair. Yet, that may solely be from old age. Jenna's Mother doesn't appear to have a connection to Mr Sutherland, seeing as they are sat at the opposite sides of the Familial Box. Of course, I *presume* they must be separated. I see Jenna look at her parents, and smile, almost to assure them of her safety.

"The battle begins in… 3… 2… 1."

Air flies out of the Domain Ball, and a grey mist viciously surrounds Jenna. She jerks up and attempts to dive over the ring of Air, yet the element wraps around her foot and slams her down onto the ground. Jenna is still, lying unconscious on the grit. Air floats above her, as if it's a spectre. The element evaporates into Jenna's body and lifts her upwards. Jenna gains consciousness yet struggles to overcome the elemental possession. Her body bolts to the side and onto a conveniently placed bundle of rocks, a shattering noise occurs. Again, I look to the screen showing her parents and see both her Mother and Father banging on the glass wall in front of them.

Aurelia is screaming, piercing through the Elemental Dome as Jenna struggles. Henry simply slams on the wall, in an attempt to save his helpless daughter from a brutal death. As I revert to the screen showing Jenna, she stumbles down to a small pond where she finds sticks and stones. The element battling her is still, as if assessing her progress. Jenna creates a fire and hurls it towards the element, causing it to blaze alight and ferociously approach Jenna. She stands up assertively, the fire flies over her as she dodges underneath. The element returns into its state of Air and surrounds Jenna, as it did at the start of the battle. A ghoulish grip reaches out towards Jenna's neck; she skirmishes as she is lifted towards the sky. I would presume Jenna's body is approximately twelve feet above the ground. Her body becoming lifeless as the grip prevents her from breathing properly; the grip disappears into a cloud of Air as Jenna floats in the sky, an immense ball of Air floats towards the body, and engulfs Jenna. The screens cut out and return to the state of reflection. I begin to bang against the wall.

I hear a scream, possibly Aurelia's.

"Oh shut up y'cow!" I hear a man say. Henry Sutherland. Amiable.

I hear a grinding noise; the Elemental Dome Ring must be getting reworked in preparation for my downfall. The floor below changes with the element colours appearing one after the other. The authoritative hologram instructing me where to stand appears behind me. I stand on the black square, and the patterned floor begins to disappear, each tile individually falling to the bottom of a hole.

"Please jump now"

Jump? Where to? I look down the hole, almost losing balance on the small square on which I stand. I'm unsure, so I wait for further instructions. The mirrored walls begin to grow closer, and I'm being forced off the edge of the square. I attempt to grip onto the walls with no luck. I need to jump. I begin to grow anxious. I look down the hole and see a red light. The lessening room manages to defeat me, and I'm pushed by the wall into a daunting chasm. I free-fall through the hole; I begin to see images of the now defunct imperials. I pass paintings of old Kings and Queens, each one looking chagrined and translucent, ghost-like. I free-fall through the hole thinking there is no end, but instead I'm protected by some sort of invisible meshwork that stops me mid-fall. A man stands at a doorway opposite me, and signals for me to come over. I stand up; every step I take creating a rippling effect on the indiscernible barrier. I'm uneasy, terrified that there might be a glitch in this profound technology and I'd fall to my death. But that's the whole point of this, isn't it? *I'm supposed to die?* That's what Ange told me to do. I step onto the hard, physical flooring and the man tells me to follow. Walking through a corridor, the man attempts to make small talk with me.

"Isaac Williams" He says. "Your Aunt and Uncle are part of the Uprisers, are they not?"

"What do you mean my Aunt and Uncle? I don't have any family apart from Mother" I snap.

"Don't worry Isaac; I'm on *your* side."

"I have no idea what you're talking about."

The man nods. He guides me through a continuous amount of corridors, in which I begin panicking. I'm shown into yet another enclosed room, in which I'm allowed one minute to organise my thoughts.

"Isaac Williams, the son of Eliza Williams, missing, and Scott Williams, deceased, born on 20th of June 2039."

I walk out into the Elemental Dome Ring. I assess the location; Claude and Ange are stood next to the Familial Box, escorted by two men and one woman. I somehow get the feeling that I'll get to know these people in times to come.

"The battle begins in… 3… 2… 1."

The Domain Ball is absent. I look around in confusion; four Domain Balls begin to float towards me.

"Choose a Domain Ball. This will provide you with your element."

I get a choice? Somebody's giving me a chance? I study each Domain Ball, looking for indicators of the element they hold, yet each one is identical. I reach out for the third Domain Ball, the three others withdraw. Water flares out of the Domain Ball. Water is *my* element. I run hastily, yet it manages to rise above me and drop, causing me to be dowsed. A fortification of Water forms around me, towering above me. As I try to walk through, a static noise is made as I'm shocked by an electric current. The Water begins to seize with electricity, this could kill me instantly. Ange told me to put up a fight. I look below me to see a rope, I throw it upwards and it latches onto a ledge. I begin to climb up; I'm shocked by my strength, so I assume you're stronger when you're in a desperate situation. I am now clinging onto a rope, probably six feet from the ground. The Water rises up and forms into a spinning ball, I jump down hoping to survive. As I fall the Water wraps around my arm and jolts me back and forth, I manage to grab hold of the rope and I swing towards a ledge. I jump onto the ledge and assess the situation; I gather that the ledge I am standing on may be a place where Water cannot gain access to me, due to safety protocols. I look behind me and see a subordinate staring through the barrier. This is when I start to die. I purposefully trip and fall straight to the ground. Water races towards me, still in the form of a spinning ball and submerges me. I am now in the ball of Water; I slash through the water in an attempt to show my desire to survive. Darkness occurs.

I awaken in a hospital, Claude and Ange are by my side, and Sophia and Alice are at the foot of my bed. My arm is in a sling, and as I open my eyes Ange begins to beam.

"Hello, Isaac. You did it. You're safe now." Ange says happily.

"You can't get out yet; you're being discharged tomorrow." Claude says.

"Where am I?" I ask.

"You're in a safety Quarter; those that are defeated by the elements are teleported here. Sometimes teleporting can be a bit off, we found you lying on a river bank near Newhaven, you were unconscious… because you drowned. Good job, Isaac, they don't have any idea of what's going on back in the Quarter." Claude responds.

"I'm in a *safety* Quarter?"

"Well, it's called the Uprising Quarter. Here we teach people how to fight, for the Uprising." Alice states "The thing you saw Sophia and I do in your dream? That was real."

I fall asleep.

Once again, I awaken in the hospital. However, this time I am alone. A doctor walks in, however she appears unconventional, with piercings and tattoos.

"You're free to go. Claude and Ange Bellator are waiting for you at their home; it's the fifth building on the street behind this one." The doctor says, her voice is gritty and unpleasant, yet I feel warmed towards her and restful.

I exit the hospital, and look to the left to find the buildings, each one featuring a characteristic somehow based on the inhabitants' elements. I approach the fifth building; one side is coloured grey while the other red. This must be Claude's home. I tap on the door, and I'm welcomed by Ange, she invites me inside and directs me into the lounge.

"It's time you had some explanations, isn't it?" Ange says, caringly.

"I guess so."

Claude walks in and sits next to me, I smile at him and he smiles back. He seems tense.

"Isaac. What do you want to know?" Claude asks, his voice seeming strained.

"How are *you* here? You're a subordinate, right? So how are you here? Shouldn't you be in a trance?" I question.

"Trust me on this, Isaac. I can't tell you that right now. There's something in place but for now you just have to trust me." His reluctance intrigues me. "Is there anything else?"

"There was this man… at the Elemental Dome, he told me both my Aunt and Uncle are part of the

Uprisers. This is where they're based, right? They're here, in this place, not the Quarter?"

"Isaac, as much as you'd like to think this, I don't *know* everybody here. Ange and I know nothing about your Aunt and Uncle, sorry." Claude seems insistent.

"How the heck did *this* even start?" I snap.

"Your Father, he... he began the uprising against Deatra. That's why you're so important in this; Deatra would kill you in an instance if it didn't harm her reputation, that's why she tried to kill you in your dream, to make it seem biological. That's why I came and wounded her, I saved you. Deatra killed your Father, Isaac. Deatra took control of your Mother, that's why your Mother is still in the Dormiton Building."

"Then we need to save her, right?" I ask desperately.

"No, no we can't. Not until we defeat Deatra, but we need to get *you* ready." Ange says, standing at the door.

They take me to a building in the centre of the

Uprising Quarter; the building is surrounded by four other soaring buildings, with a representation of an element on each of them, and another building behind. The door opens in front of me; I walk into the building to find an elevator. I step in, and see a button marked with 'EC'. Claude and Ange enter behind me, Claude pushes the button and we move to the ground floor at a relatively fast speed. We arrive at the Elemental Centre and walk into the main foyer. I glance around and see people stagger in and out of four rooms, each assigned an element. Ange directs me into an office, but as I look back to the rooms I see a girl walk into the room designated to Air. Jenna. I begin to call her name; she turns around but the door automatically closes in front of me. I turn towards Ange and Claude; Ange is now sat behind a desk while Claude perches against the window.

"Isaac, take a seat." Ange gestures towards an ill-fitting green chair which clashes with the red coloured room. "Are you aware of Warren Potes, Isaac?"

I shake my head.

"He's an Earth, but he'll be your mentor for the next week or two, in order to ordain you into the Uprising Quarter, Isaac, to help you treasure your new abilities."

"Why do I have these new abilities? What's the point?" I plead.

"There's a war, forthcoming. A battle, at least. An uprising opposed to Deatra, it's an endeavour to bring our Quarter back to civilisation, so we can live without trepidation. We plan to reintroduce the elemental powers."

"Won't reintroducing the elemental powers cause conflict? Aren't people going to exploit these powers?"

"That's a risk we have to take." Claude affirms.

"That's a risk I don't want to be part of." I retort.

"Your Father led this. You can lead this, it's in your blood." Ange asserts.

"I'm not important. I'm just a child. I'm 18, I can't

lead a war!" I cry.

I rush out, running towards the elevator as the doors open. As they close, I see Jenna rushing towards me. She yells for me to wait and open the doors. I quickly press the button and the doors reopen. Jenna thanks me and walks into the elevator, and stands next to me. It seems much slower this time, after a small amount of insufferable silence, Jenna attempts to converse.

"Are you okay? I saw you come in with Ange and Claude? Where are they?" Jenna asks.

"They're in Ange's office." I reply, bluntly.

"Oh, where *have* you been? It's been a week since we both fought the elements." Jenna announces.

"A *week*?" I ask "I've been in hospital, I drowned. Apparently, they found me at the side of a river in Newhaven, I've never even been to Newhaven. How did *you* survive?"

"We all survive, Isaac. Everybody lives. It takes a day of recovery. You must have got it bad."

I smile. Jenna grabs my hand.

"You'll be okay; you know that? Like I said, everybody lives. You can do this."

"Wait, you mean you knew? You knew that I was supposed to lead this war?" I retort, taking my hand away from her.

We arrive at the surface, and I leave without any more words said between us.

As I storm down the street, I turn back to see Jenna looking towards me appearing visibly distressed. I stroll back towards Jenna.

"What's wrong?" I ask.

"You're our only hope." she retaliates.

"Why me?"

"Stop being so selfish. These people are helping you, Ange and Claude have put *their* lives on the line to make sure *you're* alive. This isn't for you, this is for them, and this is for Sophia and Alice."

I take Jenna's hand; I smile as a tear rolls down my cheek.

"I'm petrified. But, I feel like I can't be." I feel like I can trust Jenna.

"Holding your emotions in like a man is so last century." She says, caringly. "You'll be okay; we'll all be okay."

Ange and Claude walk out of the elevator, they head to a room adjacent to the elevator and call for myself and Jenna to join them. As we approach the door, I see three people sitting behind a desk. At second glance, I notice that they were the three present at the Elemental Dome during my fight.

"Greetings, Isaac. My name is Clark Liu, and these are my associates Jay Leach and Phoebe Taylor."

While Jenna speaks with them, I try to estimate their elements. Clark has a blue streak running through his hair. Water? Jay is similar to the doctor that treated me in the hospital, only he has flame tattoos running up his forearm. Fire? Phoebe, however, has brown wavy hair complimenting her bistre skin. The ends of her hair are tinted green, and her eyes are tinted bright green.

"Water, Fire and Earth, right?" I ask, anticipating that I'm spot-on.

"Correct, you read people well." Phoebe replies, her voice is strong and commanding. "I'm Phoebe Taylor, commanding officer of the Uprisers. The other two aren't as important, if I'm honest."

"Charming yet rude. Thanks Phoebe" Jay replies. His voice is rather different, with a slightly harsher tone.

I sit in the room, perched next to Jenna and the Bellators. In the corner of the room, I see a framed photo of Arthur Allstrong, the man who adopted Deatra when she was a baby.

"Arthur Allstrong, right?" I gesture towards the framed photograph. "Deatra's Father?"

Ange hastily exits the room and marches towards the elevator looking troubled, I notice Claude looking equally as distressed.

"Oh… sorry, did I say something?"

"Isaac, we need to talk." Phoebe says, guiding me towards a door within the office leading into her own private room.

Phoebe sits me down, and invites Jenna in with me. Claude leaves, I assume to find Ange. Jenna sits next to me, and we're joined by two others. They introduce themselves as Darcy Cassano and Warren Potes. I recognise Warren's name, remembering that Ange told me he would be my mentor. I look to Darcy; she has dark red hair which compliments her olive skin tone. Warren, however, is pale and freckly, with auburn hair. Fire and Earth. I hear Phoebe talking to the four of us, yet I'm distracted by the thought of Arthur Allstrong. Jenna pokes my arm, and my focus is brought back to Phoebe.

"- Warren, could you please take Isaac to the Water Conversion room? Darcy, take Jenna to Air Conversion?" Phoebe asks the two. "Jenna, Isaac, when you're finished please head to the Reformation Building. Ange Bellator will be waiting for you there."

Jenna and I follow Warren and Darcy, as we head down the elevator I catch a glimpse of Aurelia Swan, Jenna's Mother, being led into a room by Clark. It's peculiar to see Aurelia here, as she was present at the Elemental Dome the day it all happened. I don't think to tell Jenna though, I don't want to cause her stress, particularly because we have no idea what the conversion rooms are. We leave the elevator, and are led into separate rooms, which are called Segments. The Water Segment is a light shade of blue, with the Water hologram being projected in the far right corner. I am led into what seems to be the Water Conversion room, where five different shades of blue are projected on a wall. Jay greets me, and asks me to choose a shade, and I'm told that this will belong to my elemental feature. I am given a few choices of what it can be, I decide to have my pupils tinted blue, I also have my hair tinted a teal colour, I decide to go with subtlety as I'm not fond of people giving me attention, mostly because it rarely happens.

"Interesting, Jenna just chose the same, in her colours." Jay points out.

"Well, that practically makes us best friends, right?" I laugh.

He laughs in response.

However, the laughter seems unnecessarily forced.

Chapter Four: Reality of the Elements

I wake up in a blue mist, I can hear faded voices breathing my name. I glance up to the ceiling to see blood trickling to the ground. In the far right corner of the ceiling I see Deatra, clinging on like a wild spider. Her hair is hanging down, and blood is leaking out of her purple braid. Her eyes become nefarious, and she begins to scuttle towards me. A hissing noise comes from below my bed, as I look under Deatra grabs me from underneath and pulls me down. I fall through the floor into a trench of snakes. They wrap around me until I lose my breath. I see Deatra standing opposite me, I grasp a snake and throw it towards her, and she quickly disappears in front of my eyes. My head is yanked through the pit of snakes and I land in a claustrophobic room plastered in messy paint, a golden eagle appears in front of me and transforms into a jester-like figure. The jester wanders towards me as I quiver in a corner, and reaches for my neck. I begin to float in the air as water thrusts from my right hand, causing the Water symbol to appear on my forearm. The jester rushes backwards, crashing through a wall. I race towards the hole and witness the jester fall down a dark spiral staircase. As I follow him down, I observe every step I take leaving a puddle of water behind me. As I reach the lifeless jester, I project Water to the face, removing their pale makeup. To my horror, I notice that the jester has no eyes, the sockets beginning to bleed an extreme amount until the room fills up with blood. I notice a rope dangling from the ceiling. As I reach for it, the jester grabs hold of my ankle and heaves me down.

I jolt the jester backwards and the blood abruptly

drains away, I'm able to breathe. The body of the jester lays on a stone slab, his arms and legs tied to posts keeping him still, like a sacrifice. Deatra appears behind me and forces me to the ground, stepping closer to the jester she begins to laugh as I notice she is limping. Deatra raises her hand and gestures to the right, my body grudgingly following the movement of her hand. A purple mist flows as she moves her hand towards the ground, the room begins to judder as she concentrates her hand back to me and I'm flung backwards. I ponder about a fifth element; however, I'm distracted by the impending doom. Deatra discharges an orb of purple mist towards me, I take the chance to jump forward and my body begins to fade into the mist. Deatra begins to scream, asking where I am. The mist fills the room, mercifully I am able to see Deatra, although she cannot see me. I creep behind her as Sophia appears, trying to catch Deatra's attention. Deatra begins to teleport away as I grab hold of her, we race through the threshold. She begins to claw away at my face as she struggles to break free from my grasp. We re-emerge in a room, Sophia, Alice, Ange and Claude are seated back to back in the middle of this particular one. Facing each one of them is the lifeless body of Arthur Allstrong. The four are unresponsive, yet when Deatra sees the comatose body of her Father she lets out a piercing scream that awakens them. They stand up and frantically come towards me asking if I'm alright. Deatra kneels on the ground beside Arthur's body, she raises her hand as I yell in an attempt to warn the others. Sophia's eyes darken as she turns towards Deatra. Alice follows, as do Ange and Claude. Deatra motions her hand towards the ceiling, and the four of them light up in flames. I scream out loud, and Deatra seems to mimic me, occasionally laughing. I look at my hand and it glows blue, I initially think to point it towards the flaming bodies hoping for something to happen that would save them, but I look up to see a small crack in the wall, similar to the one in the Elemental Dome where I first met Jenna. It takes me a while to decide whether I should point my hand towards the crack, or to my four friends on fire. I realise that this cannot be a reality, as Deatra would only kill somebody in a dream. If this was reality, Deatra wouldn't have set them ablaze to protect her reputation. It's a trick, the crack has been placed there for a reason. I move my hand upwards to the crack and a gush of water comes pouring through. The flames are distinguished, and four distinct piles of ash form in the room. The room begins to fill, and Deatra begins to grow erratic, dark streaks spreading through her body.

The water reaches my neck; the piles of ash solidify into four pillars that move towards the corner of the room. I raise my two hands in front of me and a wall of water begins to form. The room is now divided in two halves, one is full of water, and the other is empty. I struggle to keep the wall of water steady, pain writhing through my arms to my brain. Deatra, being on the water side, attempts to move towards me as I push my left hand towards her. She soars backwards and hits her head on the wall. She now lies on the ground in a wall of water unconscious, I lower my hands, and the water follows. *I cannot kill.* I step towards her, frantically breathing as I assume I've killed her. A hand reaches out for my shoulder from behind, I turn back to see Jenna.

Jenna's hand has white, vein-like markings that run up to her neck. Her hair has a white streak running through, it isn't tinted like I was told. She seems to be in pain, emanating a grey smoke from her hand which fills the room and clears the water. I tumble to my knees, Jenna lifts Deatra's lifeless body upwards. I plead for Jenna to stop. She looks at me, her eyes turning red. Jenna begins to hiss as her body transforms into a serpent-like creature. Deatra falls back to the ground and lets out a piercing scream as the creature lunges towards me.

Darkness.

A light shines from the wall opposite me, the floor beginning to tremble. I move my hand towards the light. A spirit-like entity rushes through my body and I flop to the ground. A door appears adjacent to my immobile body, it opens slowly, and the loud creaking noise irritates me to the very core. As I look into the room, unable to move, I notice that it is the same room as before. The hologram room, I'm able to identify similar holograms, such as Philip King. However, Aurelia Swan is no longer there. I attempt to stand, nevertheless I fall back down. My legs are exhausted; I can scarcely breathe. A gas-like odour floats around the room. A buzzing noise can be heard. This is the only noise *I* can hear. The door to the hologram room closes and fades away. The light darkens. The noise continues. I can make out breathing. It's not me. I'm still straining to breathe. I'm able to move, yet my body aches. Every movement feels like a dagger slowly digging in and out of my muscles.

The breathing stops.

"Hello? Anybody?" I ask, scared stiff of there being an answer.

An ice cold breeze abruptly passes.

"Hello?" I repeat.

I feel a presence in the room. A chill trickles down my spine.

"Please" I desperately plead. "Please, is anybody there?"

As the room darkens, I feel this presence behind me.

The breathing starts again.

I sluggishly turn around.

Nothing.

I turn back. A face. I scream. The face has no eyes, replaced with black abysses with blood seeping slowly down the face. It smiles. I scream again. The teeth are rickety. Blood covers the top of them. The face comes closer to mine. The figure falls to the ground, the pale white face slowly disintegrating up into the air. A pool of blood forms on the floor. I stand up, although I'm in excruciating pain and I'm still struggling to walk. I raise my hand. Nothing. The element is gone. The Water symbol on my forearm has faded, leaving a small outline.

I look around the room for a way out, the same door hides in the very corner of the room, shadowed by darkness. A faint blue, artificial light shimmers below the door. A sign appears.

The Surmission Room

I gently open the door, it's the hologram room. It finally has a name. Blue entities of people come and gone float in rows of six. I stroll through, for some reason feeling at peace. The holograms sputter, the noise of electricity floating around the room. The danger has lessened. The Surmission Room feels safe. Perhaps the nightmare is now a dream, perhaps all dreams are nightmares. It's hard to tell. What exactly is The Surmission Room? It contains holograms of people, that's discernible. Aurelia Swan's hologram used to be in this room, now it isn't. Aurelia Swan. She's alive, I saw her at the Elemental Centre, but she was also at the dome. She's alive, so her hologram was removed?

Then it clicks.

Amara. Amara was in this room. I saw her hologram the first time I encountered this room. My Sister fought the elements just like I did. She died. I died. Yet, I'm alive. I was told that everybody who perishes to the elements is teleported to the safety camp. This must mean Amara is alive. I begin seeking for Amara's hologram. I walk past holograms such as

Philip King, Kathryn Burris, Shae Rufner, and Raleigh Moore. Row after row, nothing.

Three empty spots occupy the row at the very back of the room. Scarlett Allen, Oscar Perry-Evans, Maria Sal-Wilma. Words are painted on the wall behind the three empty spots.

Wake up.

I'm still dreaming. If Amara's not in this room, then she's out there. She must be alive. I can wake up now.

I think back to what Ange told me, that if I were to wake up I would have needed to be in pain in the dream. The electricity still buzzes around the room. I need to find the source, if I electrocute myself, I can wake up. I ponder if the voltage would be enough. I step outside The Surmission Room, and notice a green door has appeared in the far corner of the adjoining room. I step forward, anticipating Deatra to jump out and snap my neck, but nothing. It's quiet.

I open the green door, a syringe floats in a small room. The syringe has a note tied to it.

THE RISING OF THE ELEMENTS

Inject yourself – The Bellators

Claude and Ange must have sent this through the threshold. I pick it up, and exit the small room. I roll my sleeve up; the outline of the Water symbol begins to throb. I inject my forearm, the element outline grows thicker, then turns blue. Yet, there is no pain.

Electricity. Water. Of course. I motion my hand upwards and water spurts out, the syringe must have given me the elemental power again. I re-enter The Surmission Room, and look for a source of electricity. A loose, frayed cable pokes out from behind a hologram, sizzling as I draw closer. I pick it up, and pull it out. It unravels as I take it into the room before, and hold the cable firmly with my left hand. I conjure a sphere of water with my right hand and raise it into the air above me. The giant orb above hovers closely over my head, spinning ferociously as I strain to control it. I take a deep breath; the pain will be uncontrollable. At least I'll be awake. After a few seconds of anticipation, I close my right hand shut. The ball of water drops quickly, the electricity thrashing through my body as I scream in agony.

My eyes shut. Various sequences play out. I see Ange perched in front of a painting, staring into the far distance. Somebody is calling my name. I see Deatra pacing around Phoebe Taylor, then reaching for her neck. Crack. Claude lies unconscious in his home, paintings placed around his body. Sophia and Alice sit next to each other, Sophia holds a bouquet of flowers while Alice calls my name. Mother stands in front of the Dormiton building, surrounded by subordinates. Darcy Cassano and Warren Potes are led into a cell, the door shuts as they scream. Jenna is sat with her parents, her Father faces away from her as Aurelia Swan, her Mother, pleads for Jenna to stay. Clark Liu and Jay Leach stand in fear as a shadow looms over them. Amara lies unconscious on a stone slab in a dark and irksome cave, her eyes open.

I wake up. Claude and Ange are sat next to me; I'm lying on a bed. Alice is in the far side of the corner on a computer.

"Great job waking up, Isaac. We thought you'd never get it." Alice says as she turns back towards me. "We're processing the dream now."

"Deatra was there. How was she there?" I question.

"She caught on. She knows what we're doing." Ange snaps.

Alice returns to the computer. Claude tells Ange to calm down. I struggle to adjust to the lighting, it's heavily artificial. The oxygen in the room feels limited.

"How long did that take?" I enquire.

"Approximately 27 hours. That's probably why we're all a bit cranky." Sophia says as she strolls into the room.

"Easy for you to say, you slept for the most of it." Alice retorts.

As I sit up, my head becomes dizzy. I ask to be dismissed, Claude gestures to the door allowing me to leave. I step outside, my arm begins to throb. The Water symbol is faint. Darcy Cassano taps my shoulder.

"Coming in?" She asks.

"I'll be there in a minute." I answer.

Darcy walks into the Reformation Building, and into the room where I once was. Being outside makes me feel even more uneasy, I follow Darcy back into the room. She stands over Alice's shoulder, pointing at the computer and murmuring. She glances over at me, then back to the computer. Ange directs me into a room at the back and asks me to sit. She asks Claude to tell the others to leave us alone for a minute or two, then closes the door.

"Tell me what you saw in that last moment before you woke up, the very last thing you saw."

"I saw Amara, in a cave... she woke up." I reply, bemused. "What does it mean?"

"It means we need to find a cave. Darcy and Alice will source the location of the vision. Amara might be out there."

"The Surmission Room... there were four people missing. Jenna's Mother, Aurelia Swan. Her hologram was gone. Scarlett Allen, Oscar Perry-Evans and

Maria Sal-Wilma, their holograms were gone too."

Ange takes note of their names. She assures me she'll speak to Clark Liu. She calls for Claude, and asks me to leave. Claude steps into the room, nods precariously, and then shuts the door behind me. Darcy and Alice are still murmuring in front of the computer. Sophia is sat at the side of the room, joined by Jenna and Warren Potes. Clark Liu enters the room and walks directly into the office at the back of the room, greeting Claude and Ange while closing the door. I can hear Phoebe Taylor in the corridor accompanied by Jay Leach, she hurries past but manages to acknowledge us all first.

"Scotland. It's from Scotland." Darcy utters, gaining our attention. "The Inner Hebrides of Scotland."

"Could you perhaps elaborate further?" Warren asks cynically, there is tension between the two.

"The Cave of Canorum." Alice mutters.

A few moments pass, it's quiet. I can't get the Cave of Canorum off my mind. Was it Amara? What would

Amara be doing in Scotland? Who else could it have been? Aurelia Swan? No, she's here in the Uprising Quarter. Scarlett, Oscar and Maria? Why would I be of any importance to them? Ange, Claude and Clark leave the office and re-enter the room. Clark mutters something to Ange, mentioning Phoebe and Jay, then swiftly leaves the room.

"What about the other visions? How come they're not being traced?" I ask Ange. "Claude was dead. Deatra killed Phoebe. Warren and Darcy were in a cell. How come we're not looking into those?"

"Because they were part of the dream, the vision of Amara wasn't. I've loaded the final moments before you woke onto the screen." Alice answers, dimming the lights and pointing to a screen on the wall.

Ange and the painting. My name being called.

"There, that's not part of the dream. Before the person calls your name, you can hear static. That's not part of the dream." Alice tells me.

It continues. Deatra killing Phoebe. Claude

unconscious. Sophia with the bouquet. Alice calling my name. Mother at the Dormiton building with the subordinates. Darcy and Warren in the cell. Jenna with her parents. Clark and Jay standing together. Another static noise. Amara waking up.

"See, both times there's static. When your name is called the first time, and then right before Amara wakes up." Darcy states.

"Which means that this came from somebody in the Cave of Canorum, right?" Sophia asks.

"Correct."

"I need to tell my Mother; she'll want to know Amara's alive."

"Your Mother is still in the Dormiton, it's unlikely we can retrieve her but I'll see what I can do. Perhaps you can contact a subordinate, Claude." Clark expresses this with curiosity.

"Not possible, I wasn't a subordinate to begin with." Claude replies. "But we can enquire about Eliza Williams. Isaac, what was the code for the box?"

"71390248" Warren interrupts. "Sorry, I didn't mean to interrupt, it's just I've been there before."

Clark leaves the room, accompanied by Darcy, Warren and Ange. Alice shuts the computer down and sees Sophia staring out of the window. She grabs her hand, and tells her they should go. As they leave, Claude asks me if I'm okay.

"I'm fine."

"You don't look it."

"I guess finding out my Sister is alive is a bit of a shock."

"A bit?"

This feels like a colossal understatement. In such a small amount of time, my Mother has died, only to actually be alive. I've died, yet I'm here. My Sister has returned from the dead, only to be alive and well in a cave in *Scotland*.

"I've got an Aunt and Uncle here who I don't even know. My Sister's alive. My Mother's alive. I can propel water from my hand! Sometimes, it all gets a bit too much. I'm just overwhelmed."

"In due time, Isaac." Claude tries to comfort me.

We leave the room.

I return home, I'm currently staying in a shared house with Warren, Darcy and Jenna. Alice and Sophia are next door, they share their home with Lindy Downer and Marek Reeves, who are both doctors at the Elemental Centre. Ange and Claude reside in the house behind ours.

I walk downstairs, Jenna and Darcy are sat at a table whilst Warren peers through the blinds into the garden. The atmosphere is cold, I feel tense. A raindrop falls onto the window, Warren turns the blinds and leans against the countertop. The rain is the only sound that can be heard, trickling slowly against the window. The light outside darkens. I take a seat at the table and rest my head in my hands.

"What do we do?" Jenna asks.

"This ends with either Deatra dead, or us. One, two,

or all of us, Deatra doesn't care for mercy. There's only one thing we can do." I reply.

"We have to fight. We have to overthrow Deatra." Warren concludes.

Darcy glances up with a worried smile.

We have to fight.

"What if it's a trap?" Darcy questions.

"Then we use what we have to our advantage."

Chapter Five: The Formulation

"It's off the island of Carria" Phoebe says, in discussion about the Cave of Canorum. "An Uaimh Bhinn."

"What?" I ask.

"Gaelic for the melodious cave. A natural cathedral at most." Phoebe responds.

We are sat at a round table, 'we' being myself, Phoebe, Jenna, Clark, the Bellators and both Darcy and Warren. Alice and Sophia are sat at the back of the room alongside Jay.

"How can we be sure that Amara will be there? What if Deatra's luring us there?" Claude says this with stark curiosity, lifting his head and glancing around the room anticipating a response.

"If Deatra *has* set this up, if her subordinates infiltrated Isaac's dream, then we deal with it. If, when you travel to Carria, we are confronted by Deatra and the subordinates, we deal with it in the best way we can." Phoebe responds.

"How do we remain undetected? If it is a trap, that is." I query.

"Then we deformulate the elements." Ange answers me abruptly, Jenna responds asking about the deformulation process. "Deformulating the elements means you are stripped of your elemental abilities for a certain time frame. This allows you to become undetectable for a pre-established period of time, the issue with this being that you simply become an ordinary human being."

"What's so wrong with that?" Clark asks.

"Ordinary is boring. Nobody is ordinary." Ange smirks.

"So we become nobody?" I respond.

Conversation continues, we discuss the impact Amara's return could have on the Uprising. We decide that if Amara were to be found alive, we would provide her with a leadership role within the Uprising Quarter post-Deatra if her state of mind were stable enough. Coming back from the dead must be taxing enough as it is, let alone leading a community. We discuss whether travelling to the cave would be worth it, albeit if we discovered that it was in fact a trap. I bring forth the question that if we were to be in any trouble, how would we manage without our elemental abilities? However, Phoebe assures me that there would be protocols in place to ensure our safety at all times, regarding these aren't obstructed by Deatra and her subordinates prior to the mission.

"How do we get there?" Jenna asks.

"I've arranged transport for those of you going. You'll leave at dawn. No need to pack anything, it'll all be ready for you. Just bring a few bits and bobs." Jay interjects.

"Yes, that brings me to who *will* be going. Of course, Isaac, you'll be going. Jenna, Warren and Darcy also, alongside Clark, Sophia and Marek Reeves. That leaves myself, Alice, Jay, Claude, Lindy Downer and Ange here to monitor your progress in finding Amara." Phoebe looks almost smug when she discusses who will be going where, as if it's a game for her, although I know she means well.

We disband, and I follow Claude and Ange into the Reformation Building, everyone else following. We split into the two groups for the mission to Carria. Sophia introduces us to her housemate, Marek, who brings us down the elevator and into the Extraction Room.

"When we are born, we develop the elemental gene. This allows us to obtain the elemental powers, which stays dormant until the elemental fight which triggers at least one of the elements to develop further and give us the abilities. This gene arose as a result of genetic mutation caused by the use of nuclear weaponry in the war of 1956. Now, all these years later, we use this gene to rebel against those who inflicted this on us. The innocents against the perpetrators, history repeating itself."

Marek continues to explain the history of the elements, including how *certain politicians* have tried to abolish specific elements from existence because it didn't agree with their ideals and so forth. Marek guides me into an 'extraction chamber', it's dark and bitter.

5, 4, 3, 2, 1…

A gust of wind passes over me as a needle jolts into my neck. The chamber reopens, Marek sits me at a chair. There is no pain, however I feel a slight chill trickling down my spine. One by one, the rest of the team step in, then Marek steps in and asks Sophia to flip the switch for him. He does so, and the process begins. He steps out of the chamber and quickly informs us that the deformulation will end in eight days. Everyone seems calm and collected, I feel the same. We head out of the Extraction Room and into the elevator that promptly takes us back to the main foyer of the Reformation Building. We're reunited with everyone but Jay who is preparing transport.

"You leave in twelve hours, get home and rest. You have a busy day tomorrow." Phoebe remarks.

As we leave Phoebe holds Jenna back and discusses something with her, however I'm unable to hear as I'm now too far away and they're being relatively quiet. I glance at a door that's opened slightly to the right of me, I see Aurelia Swan and the cleaner from the Elemental Dome who introduces herself as

Delaney Wax, however Aurelia Swan hastily shuts the door so the conversation is cut off from people like me who aren't supposed to know what's happening, despite my apparent importance in the running of this whole thing.

I bid farewell to Sophia and Alice, and nod at Marek. I'm still fairly unfamiliar with him. I return to the shared house next door and place my coat on a hanger. Darcy stumbles past me and out of the door with a packet of cigarettes clasped tightly in her hands. Jenna is reading in the front room while Warren cooks dinner in the kitchen. I head outside into the garden and sit by the table, I look to the left of me and see Alice and Sophia curled up together on a bench in their garden. It's comforting to see love pull through in such strenuous times. A few minutes' pass, I can hear arguing coming from the other garden to the right of mine. Alice and Sophia come over and poke their heads over the fence.

"What's happening there?" Alice asks.

"Reckon the Byrne's are having another row?" Sophia enquires.

Darcy storms into the garden and shouts.

"Bloody shut up!" She yells over the fence. She holds a lit cigarette in one hand, banging on the fence with the other.

"Still smoking, eh?" Sophia queries.

Darcy lifts her cigarette and nods, storming back out to the front of the house, Jenna and Warren step outside together. Jenna is holding her book, looking fairly annoyed at the loud interruption to her peace and quiet. Warren asks whether we should go and see if the Byrne's are okay, but I dismiss the noise as typical arguing and suggest we simply enquire at another time when the argument has died down. Sophia and Alice perch down from leaning against the fence and return to their house. Warren suggests that dinner may be ready soon, so the three of us head inside and set the table. Darcy is still outside, Warren calls for her but she doesn't reply. He brings over the dinner.

"Spaghetti Bolognese, bon appétit." Warren laughs as he pours drinks for us all.

Darcy returns, sits down and tells Warren to hurry up. Her cigarette is still lit. Jenna asks her to put it out, however Darcy pushes the cigarette onto the tablecloth and it burns through.

"Piss off." Darcy snaps, racing upstairs and slamming her bedroom door.

"I guess she doesn't want dinner then." Warren sighs, pouring Darcy's drink into the sink and leaving her dinner on the kitchen counter.

"What's up with her?" I ponder out loud, while tucking into my dinner.

"It's her brother, Diego." Warren replies.

? Diego Cassano?" Jenna queries. "One of Deatra's subordinates?"

"*Deatra?*" I splutter. I can hear Darcy's mellow sobbing in the distance. "Deatra Allstrong is in control of Darcy's brother... *Diego?*"

"That's what I just said." Jenna snaps.

"How?"

"Diego survived against Water, his element. What happens after you survive is a lottery, you either return to normality or you... you become a subordinate." Warren replies. "Clearly, Deatra saw his potential in the battle and took him into the Dormiton to make Diego into a subordinate of hers. There are occasions when the Uprisers can take a survivor, like myself. I survived against Earth, Ange saw potential so she sent Jay into the quarter to retrieve me before–"

"Before Deatra got you? Before she turned you into a

subordinate in the Dormiton building, right?" I interrupt, feeling slightly guilty for doing so.

Darcy steps back in and sits at the table with us, nobody is concerned about eating anymore.

"If we get Amara, *if* we save her, then we save my brother too. I won't let him be forgotten." Darcy says this with a staid tone, yet what she is saying seems propitious.

As Darcy becomes silent, I notice a tremor in her hand. She rubs her neck nervously; I can see that she cares tremendously.

"Okay." I reply, unsure on how to make this situation better. "We're here for you, y'know, we'll help you."

There's something about trying to comfort people, wanting your words to make them feel better but knowing they can't. Sadness is like a plague. Darcy's desperation transcends into a sadness that tears my heart into tiny fragments. She can't hear my words, perhaps her desperation and her sadness is so overwhelming that it weakens her senses. Perhaps, in her silence, she's so quiet because she's not given the opportunity to be heard. Yet, I feel guilty. I feel responsible for her silence, for her torment. I feel responsible for Deatra, because it runs in my blood. My Father started this. Who is responsible for the torment of so many innocent people? Me? My Father? Blood means blood. I'm as responsible as he is.

Darcy remains silent. Jenna looks uncomfortable, staring at the ground as Warren attempts to comfort Darcy. I cannot help but notice the hole Darcy made by burning through the tablecloth. Perhaps the smallest of things can make the biggest impact.

"Time for bed." Darcy stands up, I notice a redness on her arm.

"It's only seven." I respond, my eyes drawn to the redness. Darcy swiftly pulls her sleeve down.

"Long day tomorrow."

"G'night, then." Warren says as he bitterly clears away the wasted food.

"Keep the food for tomorrow?" I ponder.

"It's turned sour." Warren replies, scraping the food away. I presume it's not actually the food that's turned sour.

Darcy heads upstairs. Jenna smiles awkwardly, then heads into the front room to read. Warren heads into the garden, I'm sat alone at the kitchen table. I notice the burnt hole again, I touch it. The burnt edges rub off onto my finger. I stand up and head for the front door. I notice that the front door is similar to the one at home, and I'm reminded of Mother and Sophia's faux deaths, and first meeting Claude. It's been two months since I was defeated by the element. 18th September 2057. I decide to get some fresh air, I put on my coat and head outside. The door locks behind me as I take a breath.

The Uprising Quarter seems much more relaxed than the Quarter at home, despite the Quarter's purpose. I wonder about the location of the Uprising Quarter. I was found in Newhaven by the River Ouse. My home is in the Southern Quarter, if I was found by Newhaven, then, if I'm correct, the Uprising Quarter must be the South-Eastern Quarter. I'm not sure. I see children running on the street. I'm curious as to why Deatra and her subordinates cannot simply come to the Uprising Quarter and end it all, so I head to the Bellators house for answers. I begin to walk down; I can hear waves crashing in the distance. Birds roaming the sky. I haven't experienced the world like this in a while, mostly being inside or in my garden in an introverted state of mind. I turn the corner and see Delaney Wax, the cleaner from the Elemental Dome, moving into a building along with three other people. I now wonder about Aurelia Swan. Jenna now knows that her Mother is in the Uprising Quarter, she's living a few houses across us. Why doesn't Jenna live with her Mother? Why isn't her Father Henry Sutherland here?

I reach the door of the Bellator siblings. I knock four times, the door opens and I'm greeted by Phoebe Taylor.

"Isaac? Come in, come in. Nice to see you."

"Phoebe? Are Ange and Claude in?" I ask.

"Yes, yes of course. They're in the garden."

Phoebe takes me into the garden, Ange and Claude are sat at a rustic table by the kitchen door. We take a seat and Ange greets me. I ask about the location of the Uprising Quarter, and Ange confirms that the Uprising Quarter is indeed the South-Eastern Quarter.

"Look, if this is a legitimate Quarter, how come Deatra hasn't come and just, y'know… ended it all?" I query.

"Deatra and her subordinates are prevented from

visiting the South-Eastern Quarter by royal accord. Her Father, Arthur Allstrong, was part of the Uprising against Deatra and the monarchy."

"Hold on, Deatra's a royal?" I ask.

"Her adopted Father Arthur Allstrong was the last royal of Great Britain. He became bitter and abolished the monarchy, going on to form a coalition with your Father who at the time was the life monitor of the Southern Quarter. Deatra grew hungry for power and overthrew your Father, using your Mother as bait, thus the Uprising began. Deatra wishes to destroy those who get in her way so she can re-establish the monarchy. Deatra is royal by relation, but of course with Arthur being her adopted Father, she is not royal by blood. It's sick but, she has no claim to the throne. She just doesn't know it yet."

"That's abysmal." I respond. "But, how does the accord stand without the monarchy?"

"Royal accord stands until the end of reign, even if

abolished. We need to find Arthur Allstrong. He'll know how to stop Deatra." Claude says this with an uncertain tone.

"One step at a time. The Cave of Canorum, then Arthur Allstrong. Whatever's at Canorum wants to be found, if Arthur Allstrong wanted to be found he would have reached out to us. He knows we're here." Phoebe seems emphatic. "For whatever reason, Arthur Allstrong doesn't want to be found."

"By chance, does Arthur have an element?" I question the three, I'm adamant to get answers.

"The elements were introduced long before Arthur left. The royals, however, didn't receive elements. The royals and the elite were immune from the genetic mutation, but they still had control."

"The class system at large."

Conversation switches to Delaney Wax and Aurelia Swan. Ange reassures me that Jenna is aware of

Aurelia's presence in the Quarter. Delaney Wax was rescued after being interrogated by Deatra for information on the Uprising.

"Aurelia is a councillor here in the Uprising Quarter, she's looking after Delaney's recovery process. Deatra wasn't too kind." Claude sits back and looks into the window as he says this, seeming distracted.

That's all I wanted to know. I thank the three of them for their time, in return the three of them wish me luck for tomorrow's journey to Canorum. Phoebe takes me to the front door, the air turning cold.

"Isaac. Good luck." Phoebe seems to have a genuine sadness in her expression as she says this, so I smile optimistically in return.

"We'll be okay, back before dawn." I know this is untrue, but it seems to comfort her.

"Clark will be the source of communication between the two camps. If you've any issues, go to him."

I nod. As I head back to the house, I notice Delaney has finished moving in, she sits outside on a brick wall while smoking. She waves at me, so I wave back. She laughs, I realise she may be laughing as she remembers the chair incident at the Elemental Dome. Perhaps, though, I guess she may be laughing through the pain.

I open the front door; I can hear music coming from the front room. Jenna and Warren sing and dance along to the music. I stand at the doorway of the room and laugh as Jenna twirls around.

"I'm off up, is Darcy already asleep?" I feel slightly bad for interrupting their fun.

"She's in bed, see you in the morning." Warren is slightly out-of-breath, but he laughs and switches the music off.

Jenna hugs the two of us and dashes upstairs.

"You okay?" Warren asks.

"Yeah. Yeah, no I'm… I'm fine." I hastily respond.

"Sure?" Warren seems uncertain.

I smile, Warren says goodnight and high-fives me. I laugh as he runs upstairs and into his room whilst singing the song he and Jenna were dancing to a few moments ago. I go into the kitchen and switch the lights off. I can hear laughter coming from next door, it seems to be Sophia and Lindy. I switch the lights off in the front room then switch them off in the hallway. I lock the front door and head upstairs.

I open my bedroom door, the window is wide open and the wind sways the curtains ferociously. I walk over to my bed and sit down. The sound of the wind corresponds with the sound of the waves in the distance, it feels stupendously soothing to my ears. I lie back onto the bed and stare at the ceiling. I leave the window open so the cold air swirls around the room. I close my eyes for a split second.

"Isaac"

Jenna opens the door and switches the light on.

"Isaac. Wake up! We leave in an hour. What are you doing? Did you sleep in your *normal* clothes?"

I leap up and look at the clock. It's 8am. I frantically leap out of bed and change into fresh clothing. I throw some clothes into a backpack and race downstairs. Warren and Darcy are outside speaking to Lindy over the fence, Jenna rushes downstairs, runs into me and into the kitchen. She grabs a croissant and throws another to me. She opens the back door and shouts at Darcy and Warren to hurry up. The two of them hastily walk back in and stumble to the front door, with their coats hanging off one arm and their backpacks being held in their hands. I seem to be standing still whilst all this chaos happens. Jenna storms towards me and pulls me to the front door, pushing me outside and slamming the door shut.

"Come on!" She yells as Darcy, Warren and myself stumble towards the Elemental Centre.

The four buildings that represent each element, which appear in every quarter, tower over us, and the Reformation Building glistens in the new-born sun by the Elemental Centre. I turn back and see Alice, Sophia and Marek rushing towards us as we enter the Centre. Lindy fumbles with their backpacks, hobbling behind them.

We group together and enter the Elemental Centre. Aurelia Swan exits a room and runs up to Jenna and says goodbye. Alice and Sophia embrace as Ange and Claude exit the Reformation Building and join us. We all enter the elevator and travel down to the bottom floor. Ange opens a door that leads to a spiral staircase that leads down to a hidden floor. The lights flicker as all of us fumble down the staircase and into a dark and damp tunnel that goes as far as I can see.

A sign on the wall of the tunnel reads 'Uprising Station', we walk forwards as a gush of water runs below us. I can hear the elevator above rising to the main floor, the door to the staircase slamming shut. The sound of water trickling gently, and a mellow, metallic humming noise ahead of us. The lights above switch on one by one as we get closer and closer to the Uprising Station.

Phoebe, Jay and Clark walk out of a hidden doorway and greet us all.

"Home team, follow me. The others, follow Clark."

The home team follow Phoebe back into the hidden doorway. The rest of us follow Clark into a spacious cave-like room with water flowing down from the walls. He calls our names one by one, we step forward when our names are called.

"Isaac Williams. Warren Potes. Jenna Sutherland. Sophia Bell. Marek Reeves. Darcy Cassano. All here, fantastic."

I feel curious as to why the older and more

experienced Uprisers aren't coming on this mission, why have Warren, Jenna, Darcy and myself all been put on the same mission when we're only young?

"How come Jay or Ange or somebody like that have more experience than us but aren't coming on this mission? Why have they grouped together the four youngest on such an important mission? I don't even know how to fight." I ask.

"Sometimes experience can be too much." Ange's voice is beamed through speakers in the walls.

"What does that mean?" I'm unsure on where to direct this question, I cannot see Ange.

"The mission cannot be too planned out, which it would be if everyone were experienced. Trust me, if it were specifically planned out, Deatra would know." Ange and the others appear through a window that materialises on the wall adjacent to where we stand.

"Surely later on we'll all become experienced? Deatra

will catch on?" Jenna responds.

"Indeed, Jenna. But, we'll have more to work with later on. For now, experience isn't a necessity. We need you four to gain experience before we take down Deatra."

We step onto a slick carriage placed in the centre of the room, the lights reflecting intensely on its dark chrome bodywork, inside it seems to be similar to an ordinary train, with nut brown leather seats placed in rows with a grey carpet running through the aisle. Clark reaches for a screen on the wall and presses a blue button that brings in five connecting carriages which attach to the back of the train.

"Feel free to explore." Clark sneers.

Hours have passed and we all sit quietly throughout the six carriages. The first carriage, where we got on, is where Clark sits, where he operates the train, as well as the seating placed in rows which appears quite formal. The second carriage is known as the 'catering carriage', where two weeks' worth of food and drink is stored for the journey, although we'll only be gone for eight days, in this carriage is also a diminutive bathroom with a shower, toilet and sink. The third carriage is occupied by myself, Marek and Jenna., the seating is much less formal than the first carriage at the front, in this carriage there are two corner sofas placed in the corners of the carriage as well as a computer, television and music player, along with a bright yellow table with four equally as bright blue chairs around it. The fourth carriage is where everyone sleeps, five beds on each side of the carriage with an automated half-wall in-between each bed so the occupier can have some privacy if they wish. The fifth carriage is much less inviting, this being the weaponry carriage. Guns and teleportation devices are aligned on the walls, with additional weaponry locked in boxes below. Four crates with an element marked on each one are kept in the far corner of the carriage closest to the sixth, and final, carriage. In this last carriage is a large screen kept on one wall with four computers placed on desks below and a table on the other side, at the back of the carriage is a balcony with a ladder that leads up to the roof of the train. Why that would be *necessary* is something I'm unsure of.

I sit at the unnecessarily bright table in the third carriage, Jenna and Marek are sat on a sofa watching the news. Jenna turns and looks at me in a sceptical manner.

"Isaac, are you satisfied?" She asks tenderly.

"Satisfied? With what? I don't understand." I reply.

"With this, everything that's happening. Are you okay with it?"

"Of course I'm okay with it. I promise, I'm fine. Besides, y'know, this isn't about me, it's about taking Deatra down. I'm just part of this by blood."

"I don't care about the mission or Deatra." Jenna seems slightly irate. "Bloody hell Isaac, I care about you. You've changed since you found out Amara's alive."

"Might be! She might be alive!" I begin to shout, my hand trembles with rage, my breathing growing rapid. "We have no clue!"

"Isaac you need-"

"Shut up, shut up, shut up!" I cut Jenna short. "This is a blind mission, we have no idea what's going to happen and I'm really bloody scared."

"There's no need to be scared, it's just-"

"No Jenna, you're not listening."

"Yes she is!" Marek snaps. "She's trying to help and you're too busy being an uptight prick to listen to her."

I give Marek a stern look, but I'm certain both of them can see the confusion and embarrassment in my eyes. I exit the carriage and go into the second. My head throbs, my hands begin to tremble more and the rapid breathing increases. I rush into the bathroom next to the kitchenette and look at my reflection in the mirror. A pain begins to grow in my chest, I can't seem to concentrate on my own reflection. My hands and feet go numb as I collapse to the floor, my heart beating rapidly to the point where it feels like it's about to tear out of my body. I scream in agony and shout for help. Clark rushes in from the first carriage and approaches the door.

"Isaac? Let me in!" He yells as he repeatedly slams the door.

I attempt to unlock the door but my muscles grow tired and my arms fall back to the floor.

"I can't. I can't move." My voice sounds tired.

"Isaac, can you count to ten for me? Big breath in between each number, can you do that for me?" Clark's voice is calm and considerate as he leans against the door in an attempt to help me. "I'll count with you, yeah?"

The two of us count to ten slowly, I begin to calm down.

"Isaac?" Clark says this after a minute or so of silence.

I reach up for the lock and open the door, Clark is stood behind with Jenna and Marek.

"I'm gonna head to the balcony." I feel remorseful and guilt-ridden. Jenna grabs my hand, but I pull away and leave the carriage. I can hear the three of them muttering in the background. I enter the fourth carriage and spot Sophia and Warren on their beds, Sophia is by the doorway to the fifth carriage, Warren is closest to the doorway to the fourth carriage. Sophia is looking at a photograph of herself and Alice. Warren is throwing a ball in the air and catching it, repeatedly. As I walk through Warren tries to get my attention but I carry on walking, I don't want to crumble in front of the two of them. As I enter the sixth carriage, Darcy sits at a computer looking at a map of Carria.

"Isaac" Darcy looks happy to see me, but I ignore her and step onto the balcony.

I take a deep breath and hold onto the railing as the train moves. Trees race past me, but everything else seems to be moving in slow motion. I close my eyes for a second and let myself breathe. It starts to rain, Darcy comes outside and puts a jacket over me.

"Come inside."

"I'd rather stay outside."

"Then I'll stay with you." Darcy leans against the balcony as she says this.

We stand in the rain for a few minutes in silence. Darcy seems as if she's about to speak but instead holds back and sighs. She moves closer to me and rests her head on my right shoulder.

"It'll be okay, you know, no matter what happens."

I don't respond, instead I look out into the distance as the rain patters against myself and Darcy. There's a tap at the window behind us. Darcy turns back.

"You're soaking wet! Get in, come on, long day tomorrow." Sophia says as she gestures for us to go back inside the train. Darcy brushes past her and into the carriage, she tells Sophia to leave me.

I take a seat on a rickety, small bench placed on the balcony by the side of the door. The rain grows heavier so I decide to head inside. I ruffle through my hair and water sprays everywhere, Sophia pulls me in and shuts the door.

The three of us enter the third carriage, Jenna is stood at the window.

"Look at the mountains, there are people stood at the top of each one." She says this with a concerned tone.

Marek moves slowly to the window, he looks down

cautiously and takes a deep breath.

"We'll be fine." He utters.

We all sit down, spread throughout the room. Warren and Clark enter and sit at the table. Darcy switches the radio on.

Heavy rain on the Eastern border with reports of elemental activity spotted in surrounding rural areas.

Elemental activity? I presume we're close to the Dormiton building in the Eastern quarter. Marek jumps onto the seat next to me and pats my leg. I smile in return, feeling slightly bitter about before.

"If they're reporting elemental activity on the radio then it's outside of the borders, is that right?" Jenna asks curiously. "Could Deatra know?"

"It could be anything, activity outside the border isn't necessarily bad. But, people could be getting away from trouble. Deatra isn't the only tyrant around."

Warren replies hastily.

"Then why aren't we taking all of them down?" I ask, feeling slightly calmer than before and more intrigued in the developing topic. "How can we be so sure that somebody like Deatra won't come around and do what she's doing now?"

"Deatra's the last royal, nobody can ever have the same resources as her, nobody can go to such extremes as Deatra. We deal with the others when they come." Clark develops a sense of authority over us as he says this. "Enough of that, time for bed."

"What are you hiding?" Sophia asks. "You're hiding something."

"Huh?" Clark appears stunned. "It's not for *me* to say."

Sophia shrugs it off and strolls into the fourth carriage. Darcy and Jenna go to the second carriage; I approach Clark as he heads into the first carriage.

"Clark, it's only six in the evening. Why are we going to bed now?"

"You're all getting up at four, no questions." He responds. "We can't lose daylight on this mission."

Chapter Six: The Triad of Canorum

It's our second day on the train, we've spent most of the day preparing for our arrival tomorrow. It's currently 9pm, Clark has let us stay up to prepare as most of the journey back will 'be safe' according to Phoebe back at the Uprising Quarter and so we can get some rest then, apparently. I stroll into the fourth carriage and sit on my bed. Warren and Darcy are sat on their beds discussing Sophia and Alice. The two of them don't notice I'm in the room.

"Oh, Warren, did I tell you? Sophia's thinking of

proposing!" Darcy states excitedly.

"What?" Warren responds. "But Alice was thinking the same! She was going to propose when we get back."

Darcy shrieks with excitement and leaps from her bed, she begins strolling around the room, the two notice me and Darcy jumps back.

"Isaac, oh god, no. Isaac it's a secret! You can't tell anyone!" Darcy stumbles down back to her bed. "Not a word!"

"Not a soul" I respond. "Although, if it's a secret… why *did* you just tell Warren?"

Darcy leaps back up and does a spurt of jogging on the spot in excitement.

"It's just so exciting!"

Darcy begins to twirl around the room. It's a strange

sight to see, Darcy's usually quite emotionally withdrawn apart from that previous experience regarding her brother, Diego.

"I love weddings, oh my, I really do." Darcy says as she prances around.

"Darcy, are you… okay?" I ask sarcastically.

As Darcy continues to make a fool of herself, I glance over at Warren and see him looking at Darcy with a tender, loving smile. He looks down and struggles to contain it, but his expression turns sad and he appears to go into deep thought. I turn back to Darcy who continues to laugh and strut around as Jenna and Sophia walk in, startling Darcy. She fumbles back and puts herself straight. Sophia bumps Jenna's shoulder, and the two begin to laugh at Darcy who has suddenly become self-conscious and diffident.

"Marek and Clark are sorting our earpieces out; they'll join us in a few minutes."

Jenna strolls over to the window by her bed and looks out.

"The people on the mountains, they're back." She states this with nerve and anticipation. "How can they be here if we're halfway across the country?"

"They're following us." Sophia whispers. "I'll keep watch."

Sophia cautiously moves into the weaponry carriage and equips herself with a deformulation gun.

"If they try anything I'll use this, it'll drain their elements and put them into a sleep."

"How deep?" I ask.

"Deep enough. They wouldn't bother us again."

Warren accompanies Sophia into the sixth carriage, which we know as the mission carriage, while the rest of us stay here. Clark and Marek enter and give those going into the cave an earpiece. The earpieces are small metallic pieces which will allow us to communicate with Marek, Sophia and Warren while we're in the Cave of Canorum. Marek equips himself with a headset and tests the connection between the two pieces of equipment.

Marek leaves the carriage, Darcy follows him. Clark sits on his bed, Jenna says goodnight and goes to sleep. I reach under my bed and find a photo of the Uprising Quarter. It reminds me of what we're fighting for. Freedom. I fear tomorrow's going to be a big day so I tuck myself in and attempt to sleep. I can hear a muttering coming from the carriage Sophia and Warren are in, I can also hear Darcy laughing as Marek shushes her. I turn over, Clark is lying on his bed staring at the ceiling. I press a button on the wall and the half-wall separator elevates from the ground. I am now enclosed in a small box that goes high enough to give me privacy, but if there were some kind of emergency I guess I could easily climb over. I'm not sure if that would ever be necessary, though.

I close my eyes, I can still hear muttering and laughter in the other carriages. I begin to think about the Cave of Canorum. What's leading us there? Who's leading us there?

My mind drifts away as I slip into a state of unconsciousness.

Arthur Allstrong is stood behind a podium. His hands cover his face in shame. Deatra emerges from a crowd of people behind him, pushing him down and raising her left hand in the air. The sky turns a stark purple.

"The fifth element compels you." Deatra looks to the crowd behind her as they begin to chant these words.

Deatra snaps her fingers as Arthur's body begins to float in mid-air. Deatra snaps her fingers again and Arthur Allstrong's body fades away.

My eyes shoot open and I leap forward in my bed. My

heart beating rapidly, sweat beading on my forehead. I look around, it's morning. I look to the side of me, Marek is glaring at me with a concerned look. Darcy and Jenna look at me in the same way.

"Isaac?" Darcy asks gently. "Isaac, what happened?"

"The dream." I mutter. "The fifth element compels you."

Marek looks stunned.

"The fifth element? What do you mean? There's only four." Jenna responds, her voice trembling with uncertainty.

"Isaac, the fifth element doesn't exist. We've tried and tried to find evidence but it's not there." Marek seems unhopeful as he makes his bed.

"Purple."

"Purple? The colour?" Darcy asks.

"Deatra's braid, it's purple. In the dream, the sky turned purple. I've seen a purple mist in other dreams before. It can't be a coincidence."

"It can definitely be a coincidence. But, I guess I'll get in contact with Phoebe, see if she can find anything." Clark says as he strolls into the carriage.

I lie back down in bed, I presume Sophia and Warren are still on watch in the next carriage. I can't help but think about the fifth element, how I've seen hints of it ever since I fought Water.

The train grinds to a halt. I look out the window, I spot a mountain that partially eclipses the coastline. Waves crash forward, with four islands spread sporadically throughout the ocean. One island has a few small cottages on top of a cliff, underneath this cliff being a large cave. The Cave of Canorum.

"There it is. Canorum. How do we get there?" I ask.

We all step outside the train. I look around the station; a group of people stand on the platform opposite us. The station is levelled on the edge of a cliff with a fence wrapped around it. We go up a staircase and down onto the opposite platform where the exit is. As we pass the group of people, they turn and nod. They have the Uprising symbol placed on the arm of their clothing. Three turnstile's lead outside. We place our fingers on a sensor that allows us through and step out. The area is fairly desolate, although I can see a town in the distance with a road leading up to it. The sound of the waves compliments the faint sound of humanity. Clark brings us into a diminutive, pale building. He types a passcode into a keypad on the wall and the bare wall in front of us goes down, opening up to a room with a long table placed in the middle with chairs around it. On the right of the wall is a large screen where Marek, Sophia and Warren will be able to monitor our progress. A burly man comes out from a door next to the screen. He speaks with a thick Scottish accent, introducing himself as Bruce Day. He states that he's a Water element, however in this location the elements are forbidden and that they have been deformulated. Bruce takes us outside and down some rickety steps which lead to the waterside. At the bottom, a small harbour sits in front of us.

"Here's how we get there." Clark states caustically.

I raise my eyebrows in surprise. Darcy laughs as she climbs onto an unsteady boat, she trips over a bag placed on the boat and nearly topples into the water but regains balance.

"Time to go. Do you all have your earpieces?" Marek asks. "We'll get in touch via the headsets, you should be able to hear us. Clark has a headpiece with a camera in so we can see everything. Good luck."

Bruce, Sophia, Warren and Marek walk back up the steps and into the building. Clark, Jenna, Darcy and myself remain, Darcy tests the motor on the boat as we clamber on.

"Northbound it is, time to go." Clark takes

leadership, which I'm thankful for. I don't think I'd have been able to lead this part of the mission.

We sail for a few minutes in silence and anticipation. The sky turns grey as storm clouds merge together, the air turning cold and the waves growing more violent. I hold tightly on a railing on the boat as we're thrown to and fro. The cave gets larger as we get closer, but we're still quite a distance away. Clark predicts we'll arrive within a few minutes or so.

"Those cottages on top? Why are they there?" Darcy asks.

"For people who take care of the cave." Clark responds.

"Could the signal have come from one of those cottages, then?"

"More than likely. If we don't find anything in the cave, then we'll have to go up and see if anyone's around."

Clark steers the boat onto the shore, we jump off and put ourselves together. The heavy waves have made me feel quite nauseous. Jenna reaches into her backpack and throws me a bottle of water.

Clark hands us each a teleportation device.

"If you get lost in the cave, or if anything goes wrong, just use these. You'll teleport back to the others. Let's at least try and stick together though, right?"

We nod, and walk towards a small entryway that opens up to the opening of the cave. We move down a slope that leads to the shallow water.

"There's no other way in, we have to go through the water." I sigh, Clark seems most upset about this.

I jump down into the water, it goes as high as my ankles so it's fairly easy to walk through. Clark leads us into the cave where darkness transcends over us. I reach into my backpack and bring out a torch, I shine it in front of us, mesmerised by what I see. Wave-eroded hexagonal columns aligned around the walls of the cave, an extraordinary sight. The mystical blue water trickles as we emerge deeper inside Canorum.

"It's beautiful." Jenna says, her voice echoing around us as she takes out her torch and turns it on.

A small hole at the back of the cave leads to a larger area, we squeeze through and stand in silence as we admire what we see. This larger area also has columns aligned around the walls with rows of small rocks below them, the blue water seeming brighter and more mystical than before, with smoke floating above it. A yellow light shines from the end of the cave, reflecting the water onto the walls to create a rippling effect.

"Jenna, Darcy, Isaac. Welcome to the Cave of Canorum." Clark speaks with delight as he walks towards a column and admires ancient markings that wrap around them.

Darcy and I look up, the columns repeat themselves above us to form an arched ceiling, the sunlight shining through small cracks between them. Jenna's torch goes out; we presume the batteries have run out until our torches go out as well.

"Guess we have to do this without the torches." Darcy says, unappreciative of the cave's beauty.

The four of us move closer to the yellow light, but it goes out.

"Clark, what's happening?" I ask. "Clark?"

He doesn't respond, I'm stood in the centre of the cave shrouded in darkness, the blue water continuing to shine amidst the lack of light.

"Clark, where are you?" I ask again.

"Guys?" I notice Jenna and Darcy have also gone.

I turn around and see three openings, I tap my torch

frantically, fortunately it lights up again. There seem to be no markings on each opening, nothing is different about them. The inside of each one is completely dark. I stare at each one hoping for some kind of miraculous sign that will lead me to whatever it is I'm being led to. I decide to go for the third opening, which is on the right. I take a deep breath, and slowly walk through the archway. I close my eyes for the first few steps, taking a deep breath with each one. I clench my fists, take one last deep breath and open my eyes. The walls are close together, so much so that I can only just fit between them. I shine my torch around, looking for a glimpse of life on the rock walls. I reach the end of the pathway; I unknowingly step on a stone slab that opens up a bright room. I step forwards into the room, I look to my left to see a window with Darcy standing in a room similar to mine.

"Isaac, what's happening?" She says faintly from the other room. She turns and points to the wall behind me.

I turn around and see another room with Clark in, and another next to him with Jenna. The four of us, in our individual rooms, face forwards in anticipation.

"Hello, anybody? Clark? Isaac?" Sophia says through our earpieces.

"Sophia, it's Isaac."

"What's happening? Clark's camera isn't active. We've been trying to get in touch."

"I… I don't know, we're in these rooms. We got lost and separated, I don't know what's happening." I begin to panic.

Darcy taps on the window to get my attention.

"Isaac, breathe."

I take a deep breath. The floor beneath us drops and we fall into a room below.

"We've located you. You're in a labyrinth. Canorum's Labyrinth. We can't locate the exit, Isaac, I'm sorry, you're on your own. Try and find a way out, but… if you can't, use your tel–" Sophia is abruptly cut off.

"Can anyone hear me?" I ask out loud.

"I'm here." Darcy calls out from the other side of the wall.

"Me too." Jenna calls out.

"Clark Liu reporting for duty."

"Funny." I respond. "See you guys at the end, I guess."

No response. I step forward, noticing instead of wading through water I'm stood on some kind of dirt floor. As I move forwards I become paranoid of my surroundings, whisking my torch around and constantly checking behind me. The only noise I can hear are our footsteps on the dirt, I can hear Clark breathing heavily.

"What's that? Hello?" I hear Clark ask from across the wall.

"It's me." I reply.

"No, no, I know it's you Isaac. There's something else." His voice becoming frantic with trepidation. "There's something behind me. I can hear it creeping behind me."

"Don't turn around." I plead. "Walk straight ahead."

"I have to turn around. It's gonna get me anyway."

There's a loud crash, Darcy and Jenna scream in the distance as the wall between myself and Clark crumbles. I scramble over the pile of rocks, finding an earpiece and a torch. A pool of blood trickles down the trail behind me as a large pile of rocks falls from above, nearly crushing me. I leap away and fall to the ground as I yell in frustration at the now blocked pathway.

What's happened to Clark?

Did he get away?

I presume not, which may be distasteful, but the pool of blood doesn't suggest anything otherwise. I decide to continue on my journey, switching back to my original pathway. The line of crumbled rocks quickly builds up to form a wall, I'm enclosed again. I turn right, dead end. I turn back to find the pathway has changed. Two options. Straight forward or turn left. Straight forward. Dead end. Turn left. Straight forward. Dead end. Turn left. Turn right. Straight forward. Dead end. Turn left. Dead end.

"I can't do this." I cry out loud.

"Yes you can." A tall, dark haired woman in a white suit circles around me. A purple braid weaved through her black, long hair.

"Deatra."

"Ah, Isaac. Oh, poor little Isaac."

I stay silent and carry on walking forwards as she follows, calling my name in tender whispers.

"Isaac, please!" She begs, racing forwards and grabbing my shoulder. "Hear me out."

I stare at her; her eyes are a sinister shade of purple. Yet, they look aged. I guess she's been through a lot, but I can't hide the fact that I think she's totally deserving of it.

"It's Arthur, he's behind all this. Not me, Isaac, I swear." Deatra's voice is precarious. "Believe me, Isaac, I didn't do any of this."

"Arthur Allstrong is missing." I bluntly retort. "You're hungry for power, you make me sick."

Deatra begins to wail.

"You think you're so in control. You have no idea of what's about to hit you in the face, tear your life apart and leave you *alone*." I feel a rage growing inside me. "You're a pig, Deatra. You're a lonely, power-hungry, swine."

Deatra steps back, frowning, clenching her fists.

"Did Mummy never tell you being rude was naughty?" She takes a deep breath after she says this, cracking her neck. "Did Daddy never tell you not to be a girl, Isaac?"

"Did Arthur never tell you you're not royal?" I question. "Not that there's anything wrong with that."

"What?"

"Well, I guess there is something wrong with that. You see, unfortunate–"

"Shut up."

"You have no claim to the throne, Deatra." I say this as I look at my teleportation device, flaunting it in front of Deatra. "You're a nobody, *just* like us."

Deatra seems furious, rage burning through her skin. I tap the teleportation device. Nothing. I tap again. Deatra laughs.

"Do you really think I didn't know that?" She shouts. "Did you *really* think I was that stupid?"

"I mean, yeah, you don't exactly look like a smart person." I chuckle, trying to hide my fear.

"Embrace it, Isaac." She says as she examines her nails, smirking at me. "It's okay to be scared, like a little boy."

Deatra races towards me, wrapping her glacial hands around my neck as she pins me against the rock wall. She digs her nails into my neck, the pain shooting to my head. Darcy screams in the distance, the sound of her teleportation device resonating through the labyrinth. Deatra jumps back.

"There's more of you?" She asks.

I smile, I don't wish to tell her that only two out of four of us remain, I fear it would make her a bit too jovial.

However, Deatra becomes much more aware of her surroundings, looking around wildly. Her focus returns on me. She conjures a purple mist from her hand.

"You were right, you know. The fifth element. Oh, Isaac. You clever boy, *my* clever boy. You were right. Gold star for you!"

A figure comes running towards us, taking my hand and pulling me away. I look back to see Deatra was never there.

"Jenna! Jenna, wait!"

The girl runs ahead of me; she seems to navigate the area easily. I trail behind her as we skirt around the labyrinth in ease.

"Slow down! I'm not great at running." I yell breathlessly.

We approach a metallic hallway as she runs ahead and into a homely room, I still trail behind as she presses a button and a door lowers in front of me. I'm still on the other side.

"Hurry! Come on!" The girl shouts.

I try to run faster, the door getting closer to the ground by the second. I leap to the floor and slide under, the strap of my backpack getting caught between the floor and the door as it seals shut. I attempt to yank it out but it's stuck. I turn back and assess the room. It's a homely room with a mismatch of paintings hung up on the walls and a small, brown sofa with a large amount of cushions placed on it. A television is placed in the corner

"Jenna?"

"Are you Isaac?"

I turn back, it's not Jenna.

"Scarlett Allen. Nice to finally meet you. We've heard a lot about you, follow me."

She brings me into a small room with a ladder leading up to the top of the island above the cave. As we climb up, I wonder about the others. Clark disappeared, Darcy teleported back to Sophia and the others. Where is Jenna? I remember.

"Did you say your name was Scarlett Allen?" I call up as we climb.

"Yes. Why?"

"You were in the Surmission Room."

"What's that?" She asks.

"The Surmission Room, it was full of holograms. You were there, but then you were gone."

"How could I have been there if I've always been here?" She laughs as she pushes up a door and climbs out, then helping me up.

We're stood above the cave, next to the cottages I saw earlier. I can see the building where Sophia, Marek, Warren and Bruce are in the distance along the coastline by the train station. Scarlett brings me into the first cottage and tells me to wait in the living room. I sit down, I can hear an old voice muttering from the kitchen. I look down to the floor, feeling slightly awkward. Suddenly, a figure rushes out and locks me in their arms, embracing me tightly in desperation.

"Thank *God* you're okay!"

It's Jenna. She wraps her arms around me again, I can feel her strength as she repeatedly says "thank you". She leans back, puts herself together and smiles.

"You've been ages, Isaac!" She says in a frustrated tone. "Where were you? Oscar came and got me when I got lost, it was right after Clark disappeared. Oh, Isaac, you must have been so scared."

"Me? No, no, I was fine. I... I saw Deatra."

An older woman pokes her head around the corner intuitively.

"Deatra Allstrong?" Her voice is soft yet modulated. "Oh, goodness me. Isaac, it really is you."

I go cold, my heart trembles as my emotions writhe through me.

"Maxine, everything okay?" Scarlett asks.

Maxine Williams. My Grandmother. I feel like I can't

breathe, my heart hurts and my head aches. My eyes feel heavy as Maxine holds me in her arms in tears.

"My boy, oh my boy."

A twenty-something year old man walks in with a limp, his right arm in a sling.

"Oh, Oscar. This is Isaac, my grandson."

"You found him?" He speaks with a silvery, Welsh accent.

"He found me."

Maxine suddenly becomes very frantic.

"Maybe you can help, can you help? Please tell me you can help." She begs.

"With what?" Jenna responds.

"Can you take us with you? To the Uprising Quarter?

We've had to stay here because we can't use our elements, but maybe… maybe back at the Quarter you can help us use them again." Scarlett pleas.

"We have three beds on the train, we can bring you along." I reply.

"One of us is going to have to stay then." Oscar says, his voice now saddened.

"No, there's only three of you. Right?"

"You don't know yet? You haven't seen her." Maxine says this with a concerned tone.

"Who?" Jenna asks.

The front door opens, a young woman with brown hair strolls in, wearing a wet brown trench coat, with wellington boots. The woman carries a large duffle bag, plonks it on the floor by the door and looks up to see us all staring at her. She then spots me, our eyes meet.

"You must be Maria. Maria Sal-Wilma, right?"

"No, that's Amara." I mutter.

"But, then who's Maria? Why was she paired with Scarlett and Oscar in the Surmission Room?" Jenna asks.

"It's pretty obvious Maria Sal-Wilma was an anagram of Amara Williams, Jenna. Come on, seriously?" I ask.

Jenna has a moment of genius, going red in the cheeks as she grows more embarrassed.

"I knew it; I knew you'd be here." I race up to her, but she's reluctant in her reaction.

"The three of you go. I'll stay." Maxine says. "I'm not of any use anyway, I'll try and make my way down later. I promise, go."

"Are you sure?" Amara asks.

"Amara? It's me, Isaac."

"I know that, we'll have time to reunite later. We need to leave, Deatra's caught on. She's on her way."

"But… but Isaac said he saw her." Jenna speaks with confusion.

"I don't know what I saw."

"The labyrinth can give you hallucinations." Amara looks outside the window. "He only saw what he was scared of."

We step outside, Maxine assures me she'll stay in contact. I feel disconnected from the world right now, how much it hurts to reunite with two family members then to have to say goodbye to one so quickly is something I never want to experience again. Yet, I feel most sorry for Amara. To have spent her time hiding away from the world with our Grandmother, only to have to say goodbye after so long, not knowing if they'll meet again, that's a true pain I cannot know.

Although, I don't feel familiar with Maxine. She left when Father died, I was only young. Amara hadn't even fought the elements yet. I feel a confusion, the initial sorrow as we say goodbye, but the frustration built up over so long because she was never there.

We arrive at the boat, where we were before. We climb in, Maxine's stood at the top of the cliff waving us off. Amara finally breaks, clinging onto me in a desperation of tears.

"I've waited so long to come home." Amara cries.

"Why didn't you?" I ask. "Why didn't you come home?"

"I couldn't, we couldn't. We couldn't come back until we knew there was a chance of us getting our elements back, until we *knew* there was a chance Deatra could be stopped."

"Where's Clark?" Jenna asks, interrupting Amara. "Has he not been found yet?"

The journey back to shore seems much faster, and the waves aren't as aggressive as they were before.

"Why didn't you give us a sign?" I ask with slight frustration.

"We weren't sure." Oscar responds. "We gave it a try, that's how we caused the interference."

We arrive on land. A body is laid on the sand, waves crashing against it with a pool of blood trailing from the ocean.

"Clark." I shout as I run up.

Sophia, Warren, Bruce, Marek and Darcy run down from the building, clambering onto the steps in fear as they see Clark lying on the ground.

"Bring him in. We need to go." Sophia shouts as Marek, Warren and Bruce lift Clark into the building. We rush him into the train, and everyone settles down. I step outside and see Bruce waiting by the building.

"Alright?" Bruce asks.

"Bruce, there's an old woman in the first cottage above the Cave of Canorum, she's just said goodbye to her family. She doesn't know when she'll see them again, but *if* you could take care of her?"

"Nae bother." He reaches out and shakes my hand. "G'luck."

I smile, returning to the train. Before I step on, I turn back to the island. I can see her standing next to the cottage, she waves and I wave in return.

"Until next time, eh?" I murmur.

Walking back on the train, I see Clark laid across a

row of seats. Warren and Marek tend to him while Sophia switches the engine on. The train begins to move as I enter the catering carriage, Darcy leans against the counter with her eyes shut.

"What happened?" I ask.

"I saw him. Diego. I saw him and I flipped. I teleported straight out. I just, I couldn't do it."

"It was just a hallucination." I attempt to comfort her, knowing that Diego is a sensitive subject. "He wasn't actually there."

"I know, but… Canorum plays on your fears. I saw Diego."

"*Diego* is your fear?"

"He's my worst nightmare. My own brother." Darcy starts to tear up and walks into the bathroom.

I walk into the next carriage; Jenna is sat with Oscar.

"You did it. You found Amara, and we picked up two more on the way. Great, isn't it?" Jenna exclaims.

I nod, walking into the fourth carriage. Amara and Scarlett are resting on their newly allocated beds. I throw my backpack onto my bed, and sit at the end of it. Scarlett is fast-asleep.

"She's exhausted." Amara says, rubbing her eyes. "No sleep last night, she was worried. Thought you wouldn't turn up. How's Mother?"

"She's fine, I think. Haven't seen her in a while, she's in the Dormiton."

Amara sighs, Sophia comes in and tells us that Clark is awake. Apparently, he had been attacked and dragged out into the ocean but he cannot remember anything else.

We have dinner as the sun sets, the light glistening through the window as we sit and talk in the third carriage. We don't talk about anything morbid, and we don't address the Uprising. In fact, we discuss anything from the weather to the colour of the table. It may seem unsatisfactory for some, but, I guess to make small talk is to make an effort to continue conversation and prove you care. Which, perhaps in this day and age is all you can do.

We disperse throughout the train, I'm sat in the sixth carriage, which is the mission room, with Marek and Jenna. We laugh as Marek tells us how he first met Lindy.

"I was walking down the street in the Quarter when I saw this beautiful woman coming out of the hospital. She was tall and blonde; I had seen her around a few times and she was always nice but I never knew her name. I quickly ran over to the market and bought a single white rose using all the money I had. I ran up to her with the rose held out in front of me, but I tripped on a rock and fell flat on my face right in front of her. She laughed and picked up the ruined rose and thanked me, that was ten years ago."

"I guess you could say that's when you fell for her." I smirk.

"That's so corny!" Jenna says, shoving me.

"Y'know, you'd make a cute couple." Marek says, I feel myself blushing. "Why don't y'give it a go?"

Silence. The tension is unbearable.

"Oh, have I put my foot in it?" Marek laughs. "Never mind, you're still young. Plenty of time to fall for each other. Who knows, if a crushed flower worked for Lindy maybe it'll work for Isaac, eh Jenna? I'm off to get a coffee, want anything?"

"Tea, please." Jenna replies.

I shake my head. Everybody else is in the third carriage, so me and Jenna are alone.

"How you feeling?" Jenna asks.

"Good. Yeah." I reply hopelessly.

"Happy Amara's back?"

"Over the moon."

Jenna moves closer to me.

"About what Marek said, *uh*, about us being a cute couple." Jenna laughs with embarrassment.

"He's a funny guy, in't he?"

"Well, yeah but… I guess what I have to say is that if you ever need somebody to love, I'm here. If you ever need to be loved, I'm here." Jenna grabs my hand.

"I guess you'll do." I say jokingly.

I look in her eyes. It's maddening how you can see such beauty and greatness in somebody's eyes. I can see her world, and I want to be a part of it. The way she makes me feel so necessary and so at ease, my love for her is so bright but I feel I cannot tell her. She is my heaven and I am her hell. I don't wish to be a burden on somebody I'm devoted to.

She laughs as I look down, the negative anxiety taking away from the moment.

"You're enough for me." She says tenderly. "Be young, Isaac, be young with me."

With her eyes locked onto me, she moves even closer. I've never felt my heart pound so hard in my life. I notice a tear forming in her eye, I wipe it away as our heads meet, resting on each other. The warmth of her lips makes me feel whole, I can feel her cold hand on my neck as I run my fingers through her hair.

A knock on the door.

"You guys done in there? You know there's CCTV right?"

I pull away and sit back casually in a panic as Marek walks in and places a tea and coffee on the table.

"You didn't even need a crushed flower!" Marek laughs.

I glare at him, but the awkwardness of this scenario is so unbearable that the three of us begin to laugh uncontrollably. Jenna takes a sip of her tea, kisses my cheek then gets up and leaves.

"How do you feel?" Marek asks.

"I feel like I'm boundless. Everything's going the way it should. Amara's back and Jenna's here. I feel immense."

"You're a great guy, you know that?" Marek compliments me. "We're lucky to have you."

The two of us walk back into the fourth carriage where everybody else is. All the beds are full and it makes me feel content.

We all fall asleep after a while, although Clark is quite restless.

I stir awake at the middle of the night after hearing a noise, Sophia and Clark are also awake. Myself and Sophia investigate the noise in all six carriages but cannot find the source. Sophia tells me to stop moving, and moves towards the balcony. She then tells me to wake everyone up and hurry back. I race into the third carriage and quietly wake everyone up. I tell them to stay still and hurry back to Sophia.

She's not there.

Marek comes up behind me as we hear a tapping on the roof. I slowly climb up the ladder to find none other than Sophia being held by Deatra.

"Give me Amara and I'll give you Sophia." She threatens.

THE RISING OF THE ELEMENTS

The wind thrashes against us as Amara shoots a bullet through the roof from the weaponry carriage below. Deatra pushes Sophia down as she jumps back in fear.

"Could've killed me." Deatra laughs. "Your petty Sister could've killed me instead of confronting me."

Sophia crawls desperately across the roof and down the ladder. I look down and notice we're currently passing over a tall bridge with a while to go.

"Deatra, please. This isn't you." Marek pleads.

Deatra leaps over the balcony and onto the side of the train. There's an explosion in the distance.

"They're at work. My lovely subordinates causing havoc everywhere."

Marek and I cautiously try to climb off the roof as the wind grows stronger.

"Oh no, no, no." Deatra laughs. "Not today, Isaac."

She raises both of her hands and the train derails. Marek falls and holds onto the side of the train, I can hear screaming coming from inside the train as it slowly tips forward, getting closer to falling off the bridge.

"Marek! Hold on!" I yell as I grip onto his hand. "Pull yourself up!"

"I can't!" Marek cries as Deatra laughs in the distance.

"Please! Marek, I'm not losing anybody else." Everything becomes silent as I say this, everything but Marek is inaudible to me. "Give me your other hand."

"Isa–"

"No excuses, please just come back up." My grip begins to loosen.

"Tell Lindy I love her and I'll see her soon. Can you

do that for me?" I can see hope being lost in Marek's eyes. "Isaac, can you?"

I nod, trying to strengthen my grip but failing.

"Be brave Isaac. For me, be brave. You have to do this."

Marek loosens his grip as I desperately try to hold on amidst my tears and agony. He gives me one last smile as he lets go. He seems to fall in slow motion as I hear a piercing scream from below. He closes his eyes as he falls, his arms spread in the air. I scream uncontrollably as I look away, hearing a crashing noise below.

Then, I hear Deatra's laughter again. I turn back, furiously mourning Marek. I race towards her, jumping onto the track and lunge for her. She dodges while laughing hysterically. Deatra then moves her hand towards the right, the train following her direction. I look up and see the train floating in mid-air, noticing Jenna's face through a window as she screams in fear.

"Stop this."

"You go with them or you come with me." Deatra threatens.

I don't respond, instead staring into the distance as I remember Marek.

"Then go with them." Deatra shouts as she lowers the train back onto the track. "You deserve it."

I'm confused by this, perhaps she's had a change of heart despite just killing my dear friend. I climb onto the balcony and back into the mission carriage. Sophia runs up to me and asks if I'm okay.

"She's going to do something, I know it." I warn.

Proving me right, Deatra raises her fist in the air.

"Hold on!" I screech.

The train tips over and off the bridge. While we're in mid-air, myself and Sophia climb up into the fourth carriage. We make impact as the roof begins to crumble, I reach for the frame of the beds, which are fixed, and pull myself up. We make impact for a second time and I whip back against the wall, a heavy panel falls on Jenna.

"Jenna!"

No response. We make impact a third time, which causes the train to recoil into the air. Sophia is flung upwards and bashes into the ceiling as Clark and Warren fall through to the end of the train. Amara and Scarlett hold on tightly to a door as Jenna lies unresponsive under a panel. Oscar clambers into the second carriage as a door falls onto him. Suddenly, I fly backwards against the wall again, where Darcy is holding onto the frame of a bed. We make final impact as we crash into the ocean.

We are now fully submerged underwater. Sophia and

Warren break through the door to the balcony, swimming upwards. Land isn't too far away so they take Clark and go as I swim towards Jenna. I look up to Amara and Scarlett as they attempt to get through to Oscar. I try to push the panel wall off of Jenna, managing to move it. However, her leg is trapped between the panel and the door between the two carriages. I push it forward; however, I'm now losing breath. I quickly get out and to the top to catch my breath, racing back down as the train gets lower into the depths of the ocean. I manage to break Jenna free and bring her ashore. After catching my breath, I tend to Jenna. Her forehead is bleeding. I can see Sophia, Warren and Clark lying on the sand.

Darcy.

I run back into the water and dive down to the train, Amara swims past me with Oscar on her back. The train-wreck looks compacted, like a box of crushed metal and glass. I approach the train and enter through the balcony doors. I swim forwards and spot Darcy floating in the wreckage. I grab hold of her as I spot Scarlett in the second carriage with a mist of blood around her. Her eyes close as the train quickly submerges deeper, I try to swim towards her but the weight of both myself and Darcy against the speed of the train sinking deep means that we're now outside of the train as it fades into the distance with Scarlett's lifeless body. I push upwards, the sight of the crumpled train getting smaller as I gasp for air with Darcy in my arms.

I arrive back on shore and place Darcy on the sand alongside Jenna. Amara runs up to me and asks about Scarlett, but I tell her I couldn't reach her. She screams and cries hysterically as I lie back on the sand and close my eyes, my breathing growing shorter.

I find myself hanging off of the train, Marek reaching out for me, telling me to hold on. Through the train window I can see Jenna and Darcy screaming, Deatra stands behind Marek.

"Should've gone with him." She laughs. "You should've fallen with him. What's wrong Isaac? Can't you hold on much longer?"

My hand loosens as I fall from the roof of the train. Deatra falls alongside me, smiling gracefully as we plummet to the ground. We make impact and my heart goes cold.

"Isaac?"

I stir awake, my head throbbing as I move upwards on the bed. I'm in a hospital-like room. I regain focus, looking up and seeing Alice and Jay. I look to my left to see Jenna on a hospital bed with tubes attached to her, Aurelia Swan by her side with Delaney Wax accompanying her. I look to my right and see Darcy sitting upright reading a book on a hospital bed, Warren at her side with a pair of crutches next to him.

"What happened?" I ask. "How did we get here?"

"Sophia got in touch after the crash, there was a witness who saw it. Isaac, could you tell us how it happened? Nobody else was there at the top apart from you."

"Marek." I sigh.

"Isaac?"

"Lindy, does she know?"

"We'll let you rest." Jay says as the two of them leave.

I lie on my right side, facing Darcy and Warren.

"It's not your fault, you know?" Aurelia says from the other side. "We don't blame you."

Darcy looks up from her book.

"Jenna's Father, Henry. He was there, part of the riots through the other Quarters at the same time. They caught him and he confessed."

"Marek." I mutter.

"They found his body, his funeral's in two days if you want to come." Delaney tells me.

"I'll be there." I say, choking back the tears. "Give him a good send off."

Delaney says goodbye and leaves.

"What about Scarlett? Did they find her?" My voice trembles with emotion.

Warren shakes his head. He picks up the crutches, puts them into a storage cupboard, and walks to the door, telling us he'll be back soon. He tells me Amara's fine, which gives me slight relief. He walks away with a limp; he seems to have injured his leg.

I need some time alone, so I attempt to stand up. A wave of light-headedness comes over me as I stand so I gently lean against the bed. I count to five and attempt to stand again, this time managing to stay stable, so I walk outside to have some peace and quiet. I'm stood outside the Reformation Building.

The four buildings representing each element seem to be closed, perhaps a sign of respect for Marek and Scarlett who we lost on the mission. I remember that we're still stripped of our elemental abilities for a few more days because of the deformulation.

As I walk down the street, I notice that it's fairly busy but strangely quiet. I approach an area covered in bouquets of flowers and messages.

Dear Marek,

I loved you for many years, and will love you for many more. You may have been taken away from me, but my love for you will always remain.

Your dearest,

Lindy.

The message is tied to a bouquet of white roses, which was the flower Marek gave Lindy when they first met. A tear falls as I read through messages left for him, rows upon rows of flowers and notes. Another is tied to a mixture of blue and white flowers.

Marek,

Thank you for teaching me to be brave. You will always be my hero.

Warren

My heart feels heavy, knowing I was the last person to see Marek with life in his eyes, I saw him fall and it kills me. As I turn back, Ange comes towards me looking fairly different. Her hair is now a platinum blonde colour, wearing a full black suit, her eyes remaining a stark green.

"Nobody blames you."

"I can't tell you how many times I've been told that today." I sniff. "But, I was the last one to see him. I should've held on. If I was stronger I could've done something, I hate that I'm weak."

"Enough of that." Ange wraps her arm around my shoulder. "No self-doubt."

I give a half-hearted smile as she brings me back into the Reformation Building and into the hospital area. Warren is sat on the bed with Darcy, Aurelia is leant over Jenna's body.

"Please wake up. Oh my darling, please wake up." She begs desperately. "Mummy's here."

Ange gently approaches Aurelia, moving her away and taking her out of the room. I can hear Aurelia's forlorn cries as she longs for Jenna to wake up. I sit on my bed, grunting as I lean back.

"We kissed the night before the crash, we decided to give it a go." I reminisce.

"She's not gone yet." Darcy attempts to comfort me, gesturing towards Jenna's limp body.

"I just wish there was something we could do." Warren groans.

"It just takes time." Darcy responds.

"How much time do we have left, though?" I ask worryingly. "Besides, Deatra used to hold back from killing people because of her reputation. Why's that changed?"

"She's got nothing to lose." Darcy snaps. "Everyone knows how much of a rat she is now."

"Which means we're more likely to be killed." I contend. "If she has no reputation, she's got nothing to worry about."

A knock at the door. Amara and Oscar stand hand in hand, Oscar carrying a bouquet of flowers and Amara holding a pair of socks.

"Socks?" I query.

"Oh, when you were younger you used to love socks. I don't know why, it's *actually* quite weird." Amara replies, lifting up the blue and white striped socks.

"I remember, thank you."

"How's everything?" Oscar asks.

"Good, good."

"He's not badly injured, which is actually fairly *decent* considering we shouldn't have even survived the crash." Darcy intersects.

"It's a miracle. I guess somebody was looking out for us that day." Amara gleams.

"Not for Marek or Scarlett, though. Not even for Jenna by the looks of it." I whine, putting the pair of socks to my side and leaning back as Amara sits at the end of my bed, Oscar still stood at the door.

There's a prolonged silence, I look around as Oscar presents Darcy with the bouquet of flowers much to Warren's hidden dismay. He tells her that everyone is thinking of her.

"I don't mean to be rude but, why?" I ask.

"Diego." Darcy mutters. "He was caught with Jenna's Father."

"Oh, I'm sorry." I say disconcertingly, I fear this is another situation where I've possibly put my foot in it.

"Hello?" A mutter comes from the other side of the room.

We turn around as Darcy and Warren look behind me. Jenna's awake, Amara instructs Oscar to go get Aurelia and Ange as we clamber over Jenna.

"Jenna?" I approach her carefully as I hear Aurelia and Ange racing down the corridor towards us. "Jenna, it's me, Isaac."

"My baby, oh my baby." Aurelia comes running in, pushing me back onto my own bed and crowding over Jenna.

Jenna seems confused, like a child discovering the world for the first time.

"Mum?"

"Jenna?" Aurelia strokes her forehead.

Jenna takes a deep breath, wincing as she moves her arm. Ange places a glass of water next to Jenna.

"Can you remember us?" I ask, perhaps a trivial question to ask.

"Of course." Jenna chuckles.

We all give a feeble laugh.

"Isaac, you can go now if you'd like to. Darcy too." Ange says.

We say goodbye and head home, leaving Aurelia and Jenna alone. We exit through the back door which opens up to a green area. We walk down a slope and approach the sea, staying in silence for a few minutes. My heart beats rapidly as I remember the crash, seeing Scarlett's body drift away in the wreckage under the sea, seeing Marek's body fall from the roof of the train. Warren puts his arm around my shoulder as we walk away.

"There's a surprise for you at home." Warren teases.

I look curiously at him as Darcy and Amara laugh. We walk back up the slope, crunching on fallen leaves from the trees that align the way back up to the Reformation Building. As we walk down the street, we pass Marek's memorial. We stop to pay our respects; I notice that the area is still fairly busy but is now also quite noisy. Full of life. Why *must* we stop living after a friend passes? Why not honour them in the best way we can? We can remember him by using his memory as motivation for winning and living a happy and fulfilled life. I'm not certain how the others feel about this.

"Why don't we just carry on with our lives, live our lives in Marek's honour? Can't we remember him without coming to a standstill, use his memory as motivation to bringing down Deatra, right?" I ask the others.

"I guess." Darcy replies.

We set off again, approaching our house. Jenna's stuff is placed in the hallway; Warren informs me she'll be living with Aurelia. We go into the kitchen and look out into the garden. Over the fence we see Lindy planting roses in hers, Sophia and Alice come over to the fence.

"Can we come over? Lindy needs some time alone." Sophia asks.

I walk to the front door to let them in, Alice knocks on the door. As I open, I spot three figures. Alice, Sophia and Maxine.

"What are you doing here?" I shout in shock. "How?"

"Amara got Claude to come and get me, I've been here for a few days waiting for you all to *bloody* wake up!" Maxine replies. "I was in the cottage when Claude knocked on the door and told me about the crash, I simply had to come down."

"Well, it's lovely to finally meet you." Darcy greets her as I stand in silence. "Isn't it, Isaac?"

"Bless him, speechless!" Maxine laughs.

After all I thought about when we left Canorum, I'm slightly remorseful to see her again. I had prepared myself and accepted that I would never be seeing her again. Grandmothers really are persistent, aren't they? The three of them come in and we sit in the living room, I have to bring one of the kitchen chairs into the front room to sit on because all the seats are taken.

"Poor Scarlett." Maxine sighs. "When I left after Scott, Isaac's Father, passed, I went up to Scotland

and I became a Keeper of Canorum. Amara came first and we spent a year alone. Scarlett's parents lived in the cottage next door to mine but they left, abandoned the poor lass on her own with no food or money. I took her in as one of my own, she was wonderful. So very wonderful. Quite a good cook, as well, had a sweet tooth. It was just us for a few years, and then came Oscar, who was fifteen at the time, same age as her."

"My parents sent me away. I lived in a small town in Wales, they sent me up to a boarding school in the town by the train station in Carria but I ran away. I didn't fit in, but I saw some cottages on-top of Canorum and thought they'd be abandoned so I stole a boat an–"

"And you broke my window to get into the cottage even though the front door was open, silly boy!" Maxine laughs. "I was always gonna take him in, you see. I saw him sailing across on his own with a bunch o' luggage."

"I had experience with computers, I was only a teenager but I was still good at that stuff. I kept patching into the Uprising Quarter's signal and sent through Amara's interference as a sign. Thought you'd notice at least once and you did, all's well."

"But, Amara... how did you get there?"

"Um... I was in the threshold when Scarlett teleported in and took me to Carria. We'd tried to get in touch with you but we didn't know how."

"Not one day we didn't think of you, couldn't even get in touch with Ange and Claude." Maxine complains.

"How do you know Ange and Claude?" Darcy asks attentively.

"Well, they're Isaac and Amara's Aunt and Uncle. Why wouldn't we know them?" Maxine laughs, Amara and Oscar chuckling along also.

Chapter Seven: The Bellators and The Boy

I race towards Ange and Claude's house, Amara and Warren trailing behind me as they call my name and tell me to calm down. I bang on the front door as Claude greets me.

"My Uncle?" I yell. "You're my *bloody* Uncle?"

"Come in." Claude groans. "I guess it's time to tell you some truths."

"All this time you've known?" I scream, picking up a

plate and smashing it on the floor.

Warren holds me back as I reach forwards, furious that I've been lied to so profoundly. Claude paces the room as Ange comes racing downstairs.

"What's happening? What's all that racket?" She asks Amara.

"You didn't tell him?" Amara retorts as I continue to yell profanities.

"Watch your profanity!" Ange shouts imperatively, rushing over to Claude as he continues to pace around the room.

"Why didn't you tell me? My own Aunt and Uncle!" I take a deep breath, sitting on the chair with Warren next to me. Amara rushes in front of me, pleading for me to forgive her.

"Look, Amara, I forgive you. You've just come back; you wouldn't have *known* that I didn't know."

A tear drops from Amara's eye, she takes a step back and leans against the wall by the entryway to the kitchen.

"But you." I leap up, pointing at the Bellators, my veins bulge as I turn red with anger, filling with ferocity. "You should have told me from day one. How long have you known?"

"Just calm down and we'll explain everything." Claude pleads. "Please."

"Isaac, I thought it was obvious." Warren's attempt to comfort me riles me.

"Some best friend, if you thought it was obvious *you* should have told me." I retort as he raises his hands, suggesting he'll back off.

"Sit down!" Ange shouts.

I sit down, I can feel anger pulsing through me as

Warren coughs.

I drift away, gazing at a photograph on the wall of Claude, Ange, Mother and Father. Ange takes the photograph off the wall and hands it to me.

"Eliza Bellator, her name before marriage. When your Father died, Maxine kept our number to keep an eye on you. But, something happened and we lost contact. We didn't want to tell you until we knew you were ready; this whole thing has been about getting the family back together." Ange begins to get emotional.

"The day Mother died you were there, that's how you recognised her. You saw her die in the kitchen, you saw her in the photo in my room." Claude seems less frantic when I say this, instead looking guilty. "Why didn't you just tell me then, when I had nobody left? I could have used some family."

"You were vulnerable, Isaac. We've done all of this for you." Claude responds calmly.

"But you're a subordinate."

"That was part of a mission. I had pretended to be a subordinate to retrieve you. I posed as a subordinate to gain access to your files in the Dormiton Building, so *I could find out* how to come and get you."

"Did you know she was dead?" I ask uncompromisingly.

"She's not dead. She's in the Dormiton, remember?"

"Then why haven't you retrieved her?" I ask.

"We need somebody to pose as a subordinate, there's something else we need in the Dormiton."

"Another thing you've been lying to me about?" I attempt to say this with sass, but it comes out rather rude.

"Something we couldn't tell you about until we were

sure."

"The Elementarium Stone, the key to taking down Deatra and her subordinates." Ange interjects.

"It doesn't exist, surely? It was destroyed in the war." Warren exclaims, asking if I'm 'alright' straight after.

"The Elementarium Stone, if combined with the four elements, can take down a user of Aether."

"Aether? You mean the purple thing Deatra uses?" I ask, my voice starting to raise again. "You mean you knew? Another lie?"

"I'm sorry." Claude whines. "We didn't want to lie!"

"Then *why?*"

"You weren't ready. You had no safety net, you've got all these people now. We thought you'd crumble without people. You've got Darcy, Amara, Maxine, Alice, Warren, you've got so many people now."

"Reckon we'd win best bromance, yeah?" Warren laughs as he jokingly hugs me tightly as I attempt to get him off.

"How can *she* have Aether?" Amara asks.

"Aether is the rare fifth element; we only know of two users." Claude ripostes.

"Deatra Allstrong and?" I ask, urging for an answer. "Don't lie."

"Ange Bellator." Ange says, her hand trembling.

"But Claude said you had all four elements?" My anger trails into a mass of confusion as Ange sits down opposite me.

"I was originally an Air. As you know, the elite don't have elements, they didn't develop the genetic mutation, but Deatra got hold of a chemical infusion containing Aether. She had a few test runs on random civilians including myself, the others died but I survived. I had to disguise my new element by deformulating it and claiming to have all four."

"Couldn't you just pretend to have been an Air?" I ask inquisitively. "Why go to all that extra fuss?"

"I didn't want to be ordinary." Ange smirks, attempting to diffuse the tension but failing poorly.

"So what do we do about Deatra then? The Elementarium Stone?" Warren interrupts.

"Isaac, Jenna, Darcy and Warren. They're all four elements. They can combine them and the stone can stop Deatra?" Amara queries.

There's a knock at the door, Ange answers and greets Phoebe, Jay and Clark.

"We heard, Sophia told us." Phoebe says with a gentle tone.

They enter the room and stand against the wall. Clark's arm is bandaged. I notice Jay has a new tattoo of a rose on his forearm.

"We were just talking about the Elementarium Stone." Ange informs them.

"We'll talk about that *after* the funeral." Phoebe seems suddenly commanding.

"That's in two days." I groan, much to her consternation.

As I stand to leave, having taken in the news that Ange and Claude are my Aunt and Uncle, that there's a stone of some kind that can stop Deatra, and that the fifth element is real, I feel exhausted. Myself and Warren walk back to our house, leaving Amara, Phoebe, Jay and Clark to deal with Ange and Claude. It's comforting to have somebody you can consider your best friend at a time like this. I feel the same about Darcy, although my friendship with Jenna has perhaps evolved into something greater.

"My family move in today." Warren tells me.

"Family?" I ask, we're walking considerably slower than our previous journey *to* the Bellators house.

"Well, I had no idea. They got in touch today, Jay and Phoebe have been talking to them for a while apparently. *Yeah*, my Mum, Bianca, my Dad, Mitchell. My siblings too, Charlie and Haley."

"You're lucky to have your family, you sound close."

"You're always welcome in our family, pal." Warren laughs, jokingly shoving me aside.

"Any news on Diego and Henry?" I ask him. "They've been caught, right?"

"I know as much as you do, sorry." Warren replies sympathetically.

"Y'know, this might seem weird but, thanks for being

there just now. I'm not really sure about Amara, I know she's my sister and all but there's something about her. It was nice to have a friend there. Nice to have a friend through all this."

"Ah! The bromance *is* real." Warren shouts out loud for everyone to hear. "Hear that, world? The Warren and Isaac bromance is in full force!"

"Shut up!" I laugh.

As we open the door to the house, Lindy steps outside of hers.

"Evening boys." Lindy greets us.

"How are you?" Warren asks, leaning over the fence to hug her.

"I'm better, coping. Thanks for leaving the note, Warren." Lindy says this with a contradiction of strength and weakness, her voice is frail yet full of life. "Now he's gone I just have to live my life for him, ain't no time spent wallowing in self-pity. Life goes on."

"See you later." Warren kisses her cheek.

"Ever the cheeky charmer." Lindy chuckles.

We enter the house to find everyone has left. Darcy has cooked a dinner and put it on the table. I sit down, noticing an empty seat where Jenna would be right by the burnt mark from Darcy's cigarette.

"She'll be okay, stop worrying." Darcy tells me.

"I know. It's something else."

"Speak up then." Darcy mumbles while shoving the last of her food in her mouth.

"It's just, I guess, that my family have all come back which is great, but I don't feel safe with them. I hardly know them and they've just turned up out of nowhere."

"Well, we're your family too." Darcy says, having already finished her dinner.

Warren mumbles with half a small French baguette in his mouth, putting his thumb up to signal he agrees with Darcy. At least that's what I *think* he means.

"Such a pig." Darcy laughs, which in effect makes me laugh as Warren struggles to contain the crumbs pouring out of his mouth.

Darcy brings out two bottles of wine. She pours a glass, but then drinks straight from the bottle.

"Something to take the edge off." She laughs, sliding the wine glass over to me.

I shake my head, Maxine's husband, my Grandfather, was an alcoholic. He passed while she was pregnant with Father. I reckon that's why Father became a life monitor, he wanted to keep an eye on all the fathers that were never his. Darcy asks if I'm sure, and I make it known that I don't drink. I go upstairs and sit on my bed, looking up at the ceiling. The doorbell rings. I didn't even realise we had a doorbell, so I rush to the upstairs bannister as Darcy answers.

"Yes?" She asks, her sass stronger than ever.

"Hi, my name's Robbie Hart. I'm your new housemate." He spots my head poking over the bannister so I drop to the floor, I fear he may have seen me as I can hear him and Darcy laughing.

Robbie brings his suitcase in, and formally greets Darcy with a kiss on the cheek. I walk downstairs and welcome him, I put my hands out for a handshake but instead he hugs me. The three of us enter the kitchen where Robbie meets Warren.

"New guy? Better not steal my pal, Isaac." Warren says jokingly as the two combine a handshake and a hug in the most peculiar way.

The three of them sit at the table while I make

Robbie a cup of tea.

"What's your story, then?" Darcy asks, taking another sip of wine straight from the bottle.

"Well, I used to live with my family at the other side of the Quarter but they moved away because they were scared of all this conflict, especially because of my younger sister. I wanted to stay so Phoebe hooked me up with you guys. Is that cool?"

"The more the merrier." Warren says as I place Robbie's tea in front of him.

"Well, I mean, Jenna's barely moved out yet but *it's* cool." I say bitterly.

"Oh, sorry. I can go somewhere el–"

"No, no. I'm being silly, it'll be nice to have someone new in the mix." I laugh, attempting to disguise my hostile feelings.

"Tell us about y'self then. What's your favourite music, all that stuff?" Warren says as he takes a pinch from another baguette.

"Well, I like alternative rock. I guess, yeah, alternative rock." Robbie hesitates, possibly nervous I would presume. "I don't really watch telly; I find it kind of repetitive."

We sit around the table discussing all of our likes and dislikes, telling each other funny stories and embarrassing moments from our lives. I feel relaxed, for once. It's nice to live an ordinary life again. We carry on talking and laughing for a few hours until the clock strikes twelve. Warren rests his head on my shoulder, proclaiming his adoration for our 'brotherly love'. Darcy declares herself drunk and stumbles around the kitchen looking for more wine while Robbie seems genuinely happy. He smiles as we all laugh, I see him looking at us and smiling at random intervals, he thanks us for making him feel so welcome, to which Darcy responds with a slur and a thanks for being so 'cool'. I show Robbie to his room, bringing his suitcase up for him as he may have had some of Darcy's wine, which upset her for *only* a few seconds. He sits down and thanks me once again, I wish him goodnight and go into my room next door. I sit back on my bed, like I was before Robbie arrived, and look out the window. There's another knock at the door, and Warren asks if I'm in here. I contemplate not replying, although I would feel awful so I tell him to come in. He sits next to me on the bed and tells me to "budge up", leaning against me as I move to the right of the bed..

"You alright?" I ask.

"Yeah, I'm good." His voice cracks as he replies.

"You sure?" I ask, convinced something's wrong.

"It's just—"

I knew it.

"She's great, isn't she? But I'm just not sure."

Darcy.

"I really thought I liked her but now I'm just not sure. You know the feeling, right? When you think you're just really good friends with someone but you also think you might love them, yeah?"

"Is this about me, Warren?" I joke.

"Shut up! It's Darcy." Warren snaps, I feel I may have misjudged the situation.

"I know. I've seen how you look at her. You need to tell her."

"What if she doesn't feel the same?" He asks me.

"You'll never know until you find out."

"I guess you're right. Can I sleep in here tonight?"

"The bromance isn't that strong." I laugh as I push

him out, but not before he sneaks in a hug, or a 'bro hug' as he would call it.

I watch him go into his room, and I say goodnight. Darcy is still downstairs so I go down to check on her.

"You alright there?" I ask as she nearly slips over on thin air.

"Dandy." She replies, I didn't think anybody said that anymore.

"Dandy?"

"I'm old school!" She slurs, dropping a bag of flour on the floor, I'm not too sure why she had a bag of flour, though.

"Time for bed." I say as I guide her upstairs. "Go to sleep, yeah?"

She gives me a sarcastic thumbs up and shuts her

bedroom door as I go to brush my teeth.

I close the curtains and get into bed, staring at the ceiling in darkness. I can hear Darcy and Robbie laughing out loud, but I ignore it and go to sleep.

I awaken the next morning to a loud cluttering noise coming from Robbie's room. I put my dressing gown on and open the curtains. I can see Lindy and Alice in their garden, they look up and wave. I open my bedroom door to notice Warren's bedroom door is slightly open, I poke my head through the gap to see him curled up on his bed in tears.

"Warren?" I sit on his bed as he continues to weep.

"She's in his room, been in there all night." He wails.

"Have you been up all night?" I ask as I stand up and open the curtains in his bedroom, he replies saying he has.

I pull him up and plonk him onto a small sofa he has

by the window.

"Leave me alone, I want to hide away forever. My life is *over.*"

I sit next to him, and once again, he rests his head on my shoulder. Fortunately, it's the opposite shoulder this time so I don't have to be concerned over any injuries he could give me, not that it would be likely anyhow.

"Come on now, your life can't be over just because of a crush." My attempts to comfort him are abysmal, I wouldn't be surprised if I've made him feel worse.

Through the gap in the door I spot Darcy sneaking from Robbie's room back to hers. The shortest walk of shame ever, just a few metres. Although, I don't feel it's fair to judge her, I'm rather ashamed for doing so in the first place. Warren catches a glimpse of Darcy and begins to sob uncontrollably again.

"I'll make you some toast. Come down in a bit." I

sigh as I leave the room, having laid Warren onto the sofa.

As I walk down the corridor I bump into Darcy who comes out of the bathroom.

"*Oh my head!*" Darcy complains.

I give her a stern look, then smile and shake my head.

"What did *I* do? Isaac! What?" She panics.

"You'll find out sooner or later." I snigger.

"What have I done now?" Darcy shouts curiously as I head downstairs and into the kitchen.

I put some bread in the toaster for Warren and make all of us a cup of tea. There's a knock at the door so I go to answer it, seeing a peculiar array of colours through the window. I open it and a delivery man presents me with flowers.

"For Mr. Robbie Hart, from a Mrs. Marina Hart."

I place the flowers on the kitchen table, and call for Warren as his toast pops up from the toaster. He comes racing down, followed by Robbie. The awkward tension is unbearable, just as much as Darcy's awful singing from the shower.

"Good night?" Warren asks Robbie as he tucks into his toast, my eyes darting around the room in sheer terror of an argument erupting.

"Yeah, Darcy's great, isn't she?" Robbie replies. I grip onto the kitchen counter in fear.

"So you spent the night together?" Warren asks, which leads to a gasp from both Robbie and myself.

"Well, I don't think Louis would appreciate that very much." Robbie laughs.

Warren's face flares up with embarrassment, he drops his toast and apologises, to which Robbie responds by saying he understands and that he can't help being so irresistible. Finally, somebody who is even *more* confident than Warren.

"Nah, we were actually talking about you, Warren." Robbie teases. "I guess the feelings *are* mutual."

Warren becomes even more embarrassed, he attempts to put his toast in his mouth but instead hits his eyes with it, something I thought I'd never see in my lifetime.

The two of them laugh as Darcy comes in and gets her tea.

"What? No, seriously. What have I done?" She begs.

Robbie darts his eyes at Warren as I hand her a cup of tea.

"Can we talk?" Warren asks Darcy.

Chapter Eight: Elementarium

It's the day of Marek's funeral, and the day after Darcy and Warren confessed their love for each other. They spent the day together while I met up with Amara, Maxine, Ange and Claude to talk over what's happened in the past few days and to get a proper explanation of all things family related.

"You ready?" Warren asks as he comes into my room.

I struggle to put my tie on properly so Warren does it for me. Darcy is leant against my bedroom door.

"Gonna be a long day, isn't it?" Darcy says. "We've *got* to stay strong for Lindy."

"See you at the meeting later, I'll be thinking of you all." Robbie says as he walks out of the bathroom post-shower.

"Have a nice day with Louis." I respond. "Shall we go?" I ask Darcy and Warren.

I dread this funeral, I dread funerals in general but with this being Marek, and myself being the last person he saw, I dread it even more. I feel awful for Lindy too, I'm not too sure how she's *actually* coping.

We step outside all dressed in black. Lindy is stood outside, buried in the arms of Alice as Sophia locks the door to their house. Delaney Wax, Aurelia Swan and Jenna come up next to us. Jenna gives me a gentle kiss and tells me it'll be okay.

"No, no. Can't be sad today." Lindy tells us all. "Not

for my Marek. Today we celebrate him, then we get on with life."

Lindy's eyes are vacant, but her expression is so full of life. The hearse drives past, a floral arrangement spelling out 'husband', and on the other side 'daddy'. Lindy rubs her stomach as Sophia takes hold of her other hand and accompanies her to the car behind, Alice joining them. Delaney, Aurelia and Jenna enter the car behind them, Delaney being a distant cousin of Marek's.

Ange, Claude, Amara, Maxine and Oscar accompany us to the funeral service as we join up with Phoebe, Clark and Jay. We stand as the pallbearers bring Marek's coffin through and I begin to tear up. We sit down as the service begins. I turn back to see the church full of people, some people who I believe hadn't ever met Marek. My heart aches, longing for Marek to simply come back and tell a funny joke so this could all be over. Alice steps up for the eulogy.

"My name is Alice Levingston. I lived with Marek,

along with his wife, Lindy, and my girlfriend, Sophia. When Lindy asked me to do the eulogy, I thought of *so* many ways to honour him. I wanted to celebrate Marek's life in the greatest way I could. So, I'd like to talk about the good Marek has done. I will never forget how Marek guided me over the years to embrace who I am; Marek was so adamant on staying true to yourself. On one occasion, I had accompanied Marek to the hospital wing when Lindy had, unfortunately, lost her child. He *wasn't* sad, he was actually quite optimistic. He told me that life throws things at you to see how you respond, to test your bravery and your strength. Marek told me that he didn't mourn for his child, instead he was grateful for how he'd been challenged. He had a true appreciation for life, and while he did have his bad days, we remember him for being great. We remember Marek for being a hero in the darkest of days. We must remember that Marek was a good man, he never wanted much out of life but for everyone to be happy and safe. Marek was a gracious man, although the same cannot be said about the first time he met Lindy. Marek spotted Lindy from afar, and purchased a single white rose with all the money he had. He ran up to her, but fell and crushed the rose. But, Lindy saw the beauty in his crushed rose and accepted him and loved him dearly, which we must do with each other. Marek would want that."

Alice places a rose on Marek's coffin., then stepping down and taking her seat next to Lindy. The rays of sunlight shine through the stained glass windows as the sky turns blue. As we sit through the service, I admire the light shining through the stained glass, creating a reflection of colour that resonates through the church, seeming to be a sign of life.

The service ends, and the entire group head to the Reformation Building. In the main foyer is a table with a photograph of Marek and Scarlett placed on it. We go into a boardroom, the chairs and table are a matte black, and the walls are a mundane white. We all clamber in and take our seats, with Ange and Phoebe sat at each end of the table. Screens in front of each person on the table light up, Robbie and Lindy then join us and take their seats.

"Shall we start?" Ange asks.

"Actually, could we take a minute for Scarlett." Lindy asks. "I didn't know her but after Marek's service I feel like it would be nice to honour Scarlett as well."

And so we all stay in silence for one whole minute.

Maxine thanks us for doing so, wiping tears from her eyes.

"We have some news regarding your elements." Phoebe says to us all. "We're doing a semi-permanent deformulation."

"What does that mean?" Delaney asks.

"It means that for *now* we're deformulating the elements for the general public." Jay interjects.

"You can't do that; you can't stop people from using their elements." Darcy argues.

"They don't use them anyway. When was the last time you saw somebody actually use their element? They've forgotten it's there, they're *too scared* to use the elements because of Deatra." Phoebe responds confidently, a harshness developing in her voice.

"But then, without the elements how do we take Deatra down?" I ask.

"That's the thing. For everybody who decides to take part in the eventual battle, we'll give them the ability to switch their element on and off at their will." Clark states this with a sense of professionalism.

"How do you switch it off?" Warren questions. "How could it be that easy?"

"A temporary sensory fluid will be injected into your bloodstream. All *you* have to do is hold your index finger on your wrist for three seconds and your element will activate." Clark sits up straight and smartens his tie as he says this.

"Like a machine?" Aurelia queries.

"Like somebody who is desperate for peace and solidarity." Phoebe raises her voice as she stands with her arms placed on the table before putting herself together and sitting back down.

"Fine, that's fine. Right, guys?" Warren attempts to play the role of peacemaker in this.

We all eventually agree as Phoebe brings us on to the Elementarium Stone.

"The Elementarium Stone is placed in the Southern Quarter's Dormiton Building, where Deatra is based. We need to infiltrate the Dormiton with somebody posing as a subordinate, like Claude did to get Isaac's file."

"I'll do it." Darcy seems eager.

"We need somebody Deatra doesn't know, somebody

like Oscar."

"No way." Amara retorts.

"I'll do it." Oscar sits forward, his voice trembling.

"I'll go with you." Phoebe tells him. "Surprisingly, I've never met the cow."

"Deatra has an army ready. Her subordinates are under *her* control and they're willing to do whatever *she* wants." Jay leans back as he says this. "My question is… who's up for the battle?"

"I am." I quickly volunteer. "I want to fight."

One by one we volunteer, first myself, then Jenna, Darcy, Warren, Amara, Sophia, Alice, Oscar, Claude, Ange, Delaney and Robbie, along with Jay, Clark and Phoebe.

"I have a list of people who've also volunteered." Ange speaks, bringing up a list of names on the screens in front of us.

Philip King, Kathryn Burris, Shae Rufner, Raleigh Moore, Beth Golan, Emma Kempton, Matt Rochon, James Bowler, Alex Nielsen, Peter Jennings, Grace Webber, John Phillips, Wendy Chesworth, Chris Hobson, Joseph Ward, Ellen Riverson, Jordan Close.

"All those people want to help *us*?" I ask, shocked by just how many people have volunteered. I initially thought we'd only have three or four.

"Deatra has her army, but we've got ours." Clark smirks.

"A fair battle." Jay laughs.

"It's not a joke though, is it?" Jenna seems agitated by their laughter. "This is life or death; these people have signed up knowing they might very well be killed."

"Haven't you done the same?" Phoebe questions Jenna's concerns. "We *know* what's in this."

Phoebe brings the conversation back to the Elementarium Stone.

"To use the Elementarium Stone, the blood of the four primary elements need to combine to unleash Nether which will take Deatra down. We have these things called Clusters–" Phoebe transmits a photograph of two circular sphere objects to our screens.

"What do they do?" Amara asks.

"They'll detain Deatra and contain her Aether element. She doesn't have full Aether abilities. I barely have Aether abilities as it is." Ange replies.

"Then what?" Darcy enquires. "How do we get rid of her?"

"With her detained we can use the Nether to stop her."

"Stop her, how?" Maxine asks inquisitively.

"Killing her." Ange says, riddled with an abounding sense of guilt.

"Like an execution?" I exclaim. "That's sick."

"What else is there to do?" Darcy wonders. "If we leave her alive then she could easily do this crap again."

"False. Deatra can be detained by the Clusters until the Nether is ready but to defeat her Deatra needs to be released so it can fuse with her chemical infusion." Clark brings up a diagram of the chemical infusion on the screens.

"Fine." I accept Deatra's impending doom with grief and culpability.

"I guess it's the only way." Aurelia comments, looking fairly remorseful as she takes hold of Jenna's hand.

"We'll take you all down and infuse you with the sensory fluid if you're ready." Phoebe picks up her notepad and stands up, opening the door.

"I guess so." Darcy speaks for all of us, although I'm not angered by this. I feel that Darcy knows what's best at this current time.

Everyone who volunteered exits the room, leaving Lindy and Maxine on their lonesome in the boardroom. We head down the elevator and into a compact, surgery-like room.

"Your arms will go numb for an hour or two as the sensory fluid enters your bloodstream. It'll just feel like a small prick when we inject you." A nurse stands by a hospital bed as he says this, his voice sounding sharp and direct. A name badge on his shirt identifies him as Matt Rochon, one of the volunteers.

"How long until we can use it?" I ask.

"Midnight, I must advise you though, only use the

elements when it's necessary and you've had the training."

"But I've used it before, I know how to use it." I counter.

"In a state of dreaming, you have. You haven't used it in real life. Don't activate *until* you're training." Phoebe warns.

One by one we sit on the bed, Matt injects us with a long, sharp syringe. The fluid is a vivid blue colour, and when it's injected our veins throb for a minute or so. After everyone is injected, we head to the training centre. Ange brings us over to a scanner where we place our index fingers.

"To get in all you need to do is scan your finger."

We stroll into the centre; I'm stunned by how it looks. There are four sections designed to suit their element, a weaponry room at the very back with guns and teleportation devices aligned on the walls. Next to the weaponry room is a room with lockers on one side and a small canteen with tables and chairs on the other side. We walk into the midpoint of the training centre, the four sections for each element are closed off by tall, unbreakable glass walls and a door to get in and another to get out. The glass is tinted in colour to fit the elements; Fire has red, Air has yellow, Water has blue and Earth has green.

"Follow me." Ange shouts as she leads us to a door at the side. The door leads to a room with rows of uniforms, split into four sections.

The uniforms are a sleek black colour with a patch on the side of the right shoulder with the Uprising symbol on it, and a patch on the other with a specific elemental symbol. The lining of each item of clothing is specific to the colour of the element belonging to the person wearing it. I'm quite overwhelmed at how formal this all seems.

"You've had this down here for all this time?" I exclaim, not expecting the Uprisers to be *this* prepared.

"It's just some clothes." Ange laughs.

"No, not the clothes. The training centre and the sensory fluid, the stone and everything."

"We've been prepared for so long, Isaac. Now it's time to use everything we have." Claude tells me as he pats my back like I'm some kind of ungrateful dog.

"I guess we're done for today." Ange dismisses us and disappears into another room we have yet to see with Claude, Phoebe and Clark.

The rest of us walk back to the elevator, as we move up to the main foyer I can see the training centre through the glass panes, the colours reflecting on the walls, much like earlier today at Marek's funeral.

My arm goes numb as the elemental symbol on my arm reappears and begins to throb. I notice everyone else is having the same experience.

"Aurelia Swan?" A girl asks, her hair is a pastel green, which stuns me and draws my attention. "My name's Emma, could we talk?"

"Emma Kempton?" Aurelia asks, taking her away into her office and waving goodbye to us. "Is Beth around? I'd like to see her too."

We walk through the main foyer as a long queue of volunteers forms, presumably waiting for their sensory fluids to be injected. The volunteers are wearing the black uniforms that we saw downstairs. They turn to us and applaud as we exit the building.

"Wait, what just happened? Did they *applaud* us?" Jenna laughs.

"I don't know." Sophia's confusion exudes on us all. "Why would they applaud us?"

"You guys are a big deal now. You're *finally* taking Deatra down." Jay guffaws as he says this, to which we're not exactly sure how to respond. "It's inevitable, if you take her down then you'll be huge."

We arrive back home and spend the day talking about everything that has happened, from the Elementarium Stone to the sensory fluids. Robbie properly introduces himself to Jenna as the 'bedroom-stealer', to which I'm uncertain will be a name that sticks. Later that day, Jenna proposes that we go on an outing. 'We' being myself, Jenna, Darcy, Warren, Robbie, Louis, Sophia and Alice.

I struggle to get ready, unable to decide between a blue shirt or a grey shirt. I feel quite selfish about how I'm making this such a problem, switching between the two shirts every minute or so. I eventually decide on the grey shirt, stepping outside only to find Warren in the exact same shirt, so I rush back in and change to the blue shirt.

"First world problems?" Darcy laughs.

"A man likes to look good for his lady." Warren

teases.

"*Gross.*" Darcy sighs.

The three of us head downstairs and are greeted by Robbie and Louis. Louis is pale, with ginger hair and glasses, but also quite tall. He shakes my hand and thanks me for inviting him.

"Don't thank me, thank Jenna." I chuckle. "Speaking of Jenna, shall we go?"

The five of us set for a bar near Delaney's house. Alice and Sophia run up behind us and try to scare us, Warren is the only one that screams. Rather high-pitched, actually.

I knock on Jenna's front door, and am greeted by Aurelia.

"Have a nice date." Aurelia pinches my cheeks like I'm a child.

"Not a date." I laugh embarrassingly.

"Well, you're all couples aren't you? What would they call it… a quadruple date?" Aurelia says. "Jenna, they're here!"

Jenna comes out from the living room, Darcy gasps as she walks forwards. The beauty I can see makes my heart tender, to which all I can blurt out is "wow". I can hear Sophia cooing over how 'cute' we are, but Alice tells her to stop teasing us.

"Ready?" I ask, taking Jenna's arm into mine.

We arrive at the bar, which is fairly empty. Music plays in the background while a live-feed of the sea plays on a large screen. We sit around a table as Sophia orders some drinks, the bar has a rustic feel to it. Warren challenges Louis and Robbie to a game of pool, while Jenna and I sit with Darcy. Suddenly, Alice stands abruptly as the music changes to slow music.

"What are you doing?" Sophia asks.

Alice approaches Sophia nervously. She lowers to the ground, getting on one knee, pulling out a ring.

"Alice, no. Are you *serious*?" Sophia laughs.

"Told you." Darcy laughs, pointing at Warren.

Sophia pulls out a ring from her jacket.

"I was going to propose." Sophia blushes.

"You are the most–" Alice holds Sophia's hand, the ring in the other.

"–Important person to me." Sophia interrupts.

"What do you say? Will you, Sophia Bell, marry me?"

"Of course!" She shouts. "Of course I will!"

The two hug as we applaud, the bar staff applauding

also. As they embrace, Sophia opens her eyes and looks at the screen behind us, her eyes widening with terror.

"What is it?" Jenna asks, looking at the screen. "Oh my."

I turn back as the others huddle round to see the screen. I see Deatra pacing around a room, Phoebe and Claude are sat in the centre, chained against each other.

"Is this thing on? Hello? Uprisers, can you hear me?" Deatra cackles. "Look who I found! This is Phoebe and Claude, my new toys."

Phoebe struggles as Claude squirms in his chair.

"Stop squirming!" Deatra screams.

"We need to do something." I shout.

"We need to stay here. We don't know where's safe."

Sophia tells me.

"Deatra can't come into the Uprising Quarter though." I snap. "The royal accord."

"We don't know if the royal accord still stands at this moment. We're staying here."

We look back at the screen. Deatra leans against the wall.

"Do something then!" She screeches. "You're so boring!"

Claude fumbles behind him in an attempt to get free.

"No, no, no." Deatra pulls out a gun. "Not today."

My heart pounds as she aims the gun to Claude.

"Do something, Claude." She whispers, strolling to his side.

Claude sits still.

"Nothing?" Deatra unchains Claude and kicks him to the floor.

"Please." Claude pleads, sweat dripping from his forehead, Deatra pushing him back down to the floor.

Then it happens. Deatra pulls the trigger as the bullet pierces through the centre of Claude's forehead. Blood splatters across the room, Deatra's white suit tinted with Claude's blood. Phoebe screams as Claude lays lifeless on the floor, Deatra planting a kiss on his mouth as Phoebe grows hysterical.

"Shut up! Turn the camera off." Deatra roars.

The bar is silent; the staff stand there stunned as I crumble to the floor. I begin to scream, curled up in a ball on the sticky, alcohol-ridden floor. Warren and Jenna kneel by my side as they mourn for Claude.

"We need to go, *now*." Louis says, pulling us up.

Alice holds my arm as we race to the Reformation Building. I can hear screams and cries coming from the homes we pass, Aurelia and Lindy catch up as we race into the Reformation Building and into Ange's office. She's stood facing the window in silence. I call for her, but she doesn't respond. Jenna clings onto me as I clench my eyes, teardrops trailing down my face. Amara and Oscar come running in, Amara rushes to Ange and holds her as Ange's languish lets loose, her cries erupting inconsolably. The screen comes alive as Deatra reappears.

"Sorry about that. Still got one more to do." She laughs as she ruffles Phoebe's hair, a subordinate is knelt in the corner scrubbing the floor.

"No." Ange cries. "No more!"

"Tell me about the Uprisers. What *are* you up to?" Deatra puts on a cockney accent, kneeling in front of Phoebe so they're face to face.

"We're not up to anything."

"Liar."

"I guess, *yeah*. I am a liar. We're gonna kill you."

Jay runs into the room holding a teleportation device.

"Jay, no. You can't go." I plead.

"My best friend is about to be killed if I don't do anything." His voice trembles with anguished emotion.

"Please." Ange screams.

"Clark's in charge, yeah?" Jay says as he hits the teleportation device and vanishes.

"Is there somebody in the threshold, Phoebe? I can taste it." Deatra laughs as she licks her fingers and rubs them together.

Deatra approaches Phoebe and reaches for her neck, Jay teleports into the room as Deatra pulls a gun out from her pocket and shoots him.

"Even more blood, *how fun!*" She yells as she grips Phoebe's neck and snaps it, the screen turning off just as Phoebe falls to the ground.

I feel faint, I stumble against the door as Warren attempts to catch me. I can hear Ange and Darcy screaming as I fall into Warren's arms, my eyes closing as I descend into a state of unconsciousness.

I find myself in the Surmission Room, the holograms have gone, although one remains. I approach the hologram as it rotates to face me. I look at a sign to the right of the hologram.

Eliza Williams

The hologram of Mother faces me, I step back as I notice the eyes on the hologram have been hollowed out. Mother walks in through the door behind me.

"Isaac, be brave. I've passed on but please, for me and your Father, be brave. Tell Amara I love her." Her voice is soothing. "Heaven is such a lovely place; I love you Isaac."

I wake up in my bed; Amara, Jenna and Warren by my side. Jenna holds my hand as Amara tells me that Mother has been found drowned in a river.

"I know." I respond, too emotionally drained to grieve. "I saw her, she said she loved you."

"Ange is in a bad state; you both might want to go and see her." Warren tells us.

"I guess, yeah, might distract me for a while until Oscar comes back."

"Oscar? Where's he gone?" I ask.

"He's with Deatra. You know, pretending to be a subordinate so he can get the Elementarium Stone."

Amara exhales.

"Oh gosh." I respond, my voice is tired and empty.

"We can check in on her before we go to training." Jenna suggests. "Come on, Isaac. Get up, we should go."

I sit up, Jenna and Amara leave the room. Warren asks if I'm okay as Darcy pops her head round the door, rushes in and locks me in her arms.

"Come on, you should get dressed." Darcy says as she squeezes tightly.

The two leave the room, I throw on some clothes from a pile in the corner of my room. I'm curious about the sensory fluids, so I enter the bathroom and press my index finger against my wrist for three seconds. To my surprise, a jet of water spurts from my hand. I'm able to control it more, directing it straight into the sink. I notice the elemental symbol for Water is now a permanent addition to my arm. I conjure a small ball of water and direct it to my face. A much easier way to wash my face, I guess. I head downstairs as Robbie hands me a bottle of water. We make our way to Ange's house while on the way to the Reformation Building. The colour that was painted on the house before is now a dull grey colour. I knock on the door, but there's no answer. The door is unlocked so I call out for Ange. The others wait outside while Amara and I cautiously walk into the house. We find Ange sat in the living room, with no furniture but the stool she's sat on. She's perched in front of an easel with a painting of the coastline, her clothes splattered with a variety of coloured paint. To the side of Ange is a portrait of Claude, and on the other side is a portrait of Mother.

"Auntie Ange." Amara calls out gently. "It's Amara and Isaac."

Ange doesn't respond, instead sitting blank-faced in front of the easel. She finally moves, but only to add to the painting in front of her. We tell her we'll see her later, still with no response.

"She's not good." I tell the others as we close the front door.

"Bless her. Lost her sister and her brother." Robbie sighs.

"Come on, we should go." Warren says.

We enter the Reformation Building where the table with Marek and Scarlett's photos are adorned in flowers and letters. In addition to their photos are photographs of Claude, Phoebe and Jay. We enter Ange's office to find Lindy sitting at the desk.

"They've put me in charge, Clark's with Oscar right now so *me* and Aurelia are in charge." Lindy fumbles. "Oh, they're waiting for you, by the way."

"Who? Who else could be there?" I ask, I wonder this because everyone who's important is either dead or busy.

"It says here, hold on." Lindy looks through a pile of papers. "Beth Golan, Emma Kempton, Matt Rochon and Alex Nielsen."

"The volunteers?" Darcy asks Lindy, taking the paper to look at herself.

"Apparently they have experience with the elements."

We head to the training centre, leaving Lindy in Ange's office as Aurelia goes in with more paperwork.

We're greeted by the four newcomers, and split into our elements. Robbie, Jenna and Sophia go into Air with Alex. Darcy, Alice and Delaney, who joins us late, go into Fire with Beth. Lindy, Maxine and Aurelia then come into the training centre, telling us that they'd like to take part.

"Who's looking after upstairs?" I ask.

"Some of the volunteers, James and Shae are already fully trained so they were willing to look after it all."

Amara, Maxine and Warren go with Matt to Earth, while Lindy, Aurelia and I go to Water with Emma. In each compartment of the training centre are volunteers who are already training. I head to the canteen to put my bottle of water away as a person my age approaches me.

"Thanks for letting us help out." He says. "I'm Peter Jennings, nice to *finally* meet you."

"You too." I say as he smiles, heading back to the canteen.

The doors to the training centre open as Oscar and Clark walk in.

"Oscar, your face!" Amara shrieks, Oscar's face is scarred and his clothing is tattered and torn.

"He got it, though." Clark laughs. "We've put the Elementarium Stone in a safe place until we need it."

"How?" I ask.

"Well, Deatra caught on. I mean, I did a good job pretending to be a subordinate, I made it all the way into the Dormiton and underground into the vault when the alarm went off. Clark teleported in and got hold of me and teleported us away."

"That was *after* he was attacked by a bunch of ravenous subordinates." Clark laughs, referring to Oscar's scar. "They're stronger now, but fortunately *this* guy had been doing some late night Earth training so he was prepared. There was only one subordinate left when I got there."

We begin training, Emma teaches me how to control and adapt the element. I can now conjure a ball of water and project it to a target. I can also shoot miniscule pellets of water, that I can say from personal experience definitely *does* hurt. Darcy can now conjure flames and fireballs, Warren can make the ground tremble and lift rocks with no contact, and Jenna can cause tornadoes and throw people around. I must admit, it does sound very surreal, which makes it all the more wonderful.

We spend the evening in the training centre talking about how we would combine elements. Myself and Darcy stand up in the middle of the centre as I shoot a jet of water to the ground and she shoots a flame causing smoke to appear. We're taught that combining our elements is an advantage in battle.

"Think we're ready?" Maxine laughs.

"Maybe after a month or two."

Chapter Nine: The Battle of The Elements

We've been training for a *very* long time; by this I mean a few months, one or two at maximum, so actually *not* that long. We took a break for Christmas and the New Year, but now we're prepared to fight Deatra. We had a memorial service for Claude, Phoebe and Jay. Ange is almost back to her normal self, but she's still distant, although she painted portraits of the three of them for the service. Warren and Darcy, myself and Jenna, and Alice and Sophia are stronger than ever. But, Robbie and Louis have separated. We spent the day after they split comforting Robbie, we baked cakes and, *truthfully*, ate a lot of food. I guess I'm not complaining, though. Not a lot has really happened, otherwise. We've spent most of our time perfecting our elements, it *feels* epic. Being able to do such amazing things is both exhilarating *and* annihilating, knowing just how much devastation these abilities could cause if somebody were hateful enough to use their abilities for bad. Although, I guess that's been done before with politicians all over the world.

Despite how strong we've grown; I still fear the inevitable battle. We're set to depart in two days for the Southern Quarter. I'm currently sat in the Elemental Centre where we're set to plan our attack. I can see the Reformation Building glistening in the winter sunlight, the remains of snow on the ground shining by a memorial fountain we've built for Marek, Scarlett, Phoebe, Jay and Claude. Although, I do fear that the memorial will be there to remember some more people after the battle. At least, Clark's warned us that casualties are inevitable.

"Here you go." Warren says, handing me a cup of tea.

"Thanks."

"Everything okay?" He asks, nudging my shoulder. "You scared?"

"I guess I just don't want to lose anyone else."

"Is this the bromance again?" Warren jokes.

"Be serious, in two days we might not be here."

"Sorry, I guess I'm just *scared* too. I don't want to admit it." Warren began. "There are things we're gonna do that we're not proud of, but it's a risk we have to take. If we lose people, then we lose them fighting for peace and freedom. I don't know, I'm scared but I'm proud."

"Why are you proud?" I question him.

"Proud because we're fighting for what we believe

in."

"Even if we die, though?"

"Isaac, I'm willing to die fighting for what I believe in." Warren looks at me sternly. "If you're going to question that then you can go. Don't bother fighting in this if you don't care about it."

"I'm sorry. I jus–"

"Shall we go in?" Darcy asks as she and Jenna enter the Elemental Centre, followed by Sophia, Alice, Clark and Robbie.

We enter a room with a box laid in the centre. Lindy, Aurelia, and Delaney stand by the side. Amara, Maxine and Oscar follow behind us.

"Open it." Aurelia instructs us.

Jenna and I go up to the box and unlatch it, as it opens two balls float up into the air and hover.

"Clusters." Clark says. "What we use to detain Deatra."

"Clusters." I repeat.

"We're moving the attack up to tomorrow." Delaney tells us.

"How come? We're *not* ready." I ask belligerently.

"We're ready."

My hands begin to tremble, I take a deep breath and count to ten as Jenna takes hold of my hand.

"Okay, ready."

"Up at four. We'll have to go in early, use time to our advantage." Clark proposes.

We put the Clusters back into the box, and take it with us on the way home. Jenna decides to stay at ours while Aurelia spends the night at the Reformation Building assisting the volunteers.

We spend the night talking about those we've lost. We talk about how it was Marek that brought us together, and how it was Phoebe and Jay that held the operation together. We remember Scarlett being so kind, and we remember Claude being the one who started all of this. We go up to bed as the sky darkens and the temperature outside drops. Jenna gets into bed as I look outside, seeing Lindy tend to the garden. She kneels by a birdbath and looks up at the sky, she turns back and waves at me as Sophia and Alice take her inside. The Uprising Quarter is silent, almost in mourning. The lights in houses go out one by one, until my bedroom is the only one left.

"Goodbye." I mutter as I close the curtains.

I go to the light switch and stand there, my hand hovering over it. I look at Jenna who is already asleep, her gentle snoring doesn't bother me. I turn the light off and climb into bed. I nestle up to Jenna's warm body as I drift into a sleep.

"Isaac, be brave." Mother calls out. "Protect the ones you love. Tell Amara I love her."

"Darcy!" Warren screams as he fumbles over her lifeless body, kissing her forehead in tears.

Aurelia emerges from the darkness, Henry Sutherland trailing behind her.

"Aurelia, please! Listen to me." He shouts. "I didn't mean to do it."

"It's too late." Aurelia hisses.

Henry grabs Aurelia and pushes her against a wall. Aurelia knees him as he lunges for her, she runs into the darkness as Delaney Wax shoots Henry. She kneels by his lifeless body as blood trickles across the floor, Deatra emerging behind her and raising her hand in the air. Delaney begins to hover in mid-air, Deatra violently drops her hand as Delaney's body slams against the floor, head first. Sophia and Alice stand at an altar as they get married. They look behind them to find their guests all dead. Alice turns back as Sophia pushes her back, her body lowers to the ground leaving a smear of blood on the white wall.

I hear an alarm going off in the distance, and that's when I wake up.

It's four in the morning, the day we face Deatra. It feels anomalously calm as I notice an orange flickering light shining into the bedroom. It shouldn't be light this early. I race to the windows and thrash open the curtains. The Reformation Building is on fire.

"Jenna! Wake up!" I yell. "It's happening."

Darcy and Robbie come running in.

"We need to go, *now*." Darcy tells us calmly, contradictive to what's happening outside.

A helicopter lands in front of our house as all five of us rush down the stairs. Sophia, Alice and Lindy run out of their house as we clamber on to the helicopter.

"Get on!" I yell as we help them up.

Fortunately, Clark told us to wear our Uprising uniforms when we slept because he wasn't sure if there would be an attack. *Fortunately*, he was correct. The helicopter takes off as subordinates race below us with guns, shooting at us. The helicopter swerves through the crumbling Reformation Building, smashing through the glass windows of the Elemental Centre. Another helicopter flies past us with Amara and the others inside. I turn to my left to see yet another two helicopters with the volunteers inside. Alex points to his wrist and activates his element, so we all do the same. When we activate the elements, the elemental symbol marking throbs for a second or so.

The helicopter is silent as I look behind us and see the Reformation Building burning. Flames erupt as a tornado emerges from the coastline. I see an array of elements being thrashed around as I see tiny specks of subordinates fighting the civilians of the Uprising Quarter as we fly closer to our impending doom.

"Can anyone hear me? The subordinates have taken the Elementarium Stone." Clark's voice is beamed through speakers in the helicopter. "The Elementarium Stone is back in the custody of Deatra."

"One more thing to get I suppose." I say, my breathing growing more rapid.

"Get ready to run." Alice shouts as we get closer to the Southern Quarter, missiles being shot from the helicopter to a group of subordinates at the border.

"Isaac, I love you." Jenna kisses me.

"I love you too."

We land at a fairly desolate area of the Southern

Quarter. Smoke rises in the distance. We climb off and assess our surroundings.

"It's like a ghost town." Amara says as she steps off the helicopter. "It wasn't like this before."

The ground trembles below as we run forwards into the centre of the Southern Quarter.

"Where is everyone?" Darcy asks.

Deatra walks forward out of the Dormiton, Henry Sutherland and Diego Cassano by her side.

"I don't want to fight." Deatra says, the sound of her voice sending chills down my neck.

We all stand ready to battle as the volunteer helicopters land across from us. The groups emerging and standing still as subordinates surround them.

"I just want to talk." Deatra laughs.

"About what?" I say as I spit in her face.

"Why did *you* steal my stone?" She screeches as she strikes me and I fall to the ground.

Deatra walks to the front of the Dormiton Building as the Uprisers surround her.

"Well, if you're not going to be nice." Deatra shouts, her tone is comedic yet distasteful.

The volunteers begin to riot, and so do we. I push a subordinate out of the way as the battle begins. A subordinate lunges for me as I eject a heavy stream of water that Darcy counters to fill the area with smoke. Warren raises his hands as he lifts a rock, it hovers in his hands as he flicks upwards and it shoots towards a subordinate.

"Ah, the elements have risen." Deatra laughs. "Too bad."

Myself, Darcy, Warren and Jenna race through the

battle as we approach Diego.

He pulls a gun out.

"No elements here." Diego says snidely.

A purple mist flows through the scene. My arm is in agony as I drop to the floor. I can hear Deatra's pompous laughing in the distance.

"For Marek." I shout as Jenna races towards Deatra and tackles her to the ground.

"Jenna!" I yell.

Deatra and Jenna tussle in a fist fight until Deatra levitates Jenna's body and throws her into the crowd. I lift Jenna's body up as we run into a forest, chased by Deatra and her subordinates.

"Darcy, do something!" Aurelia begs.

Darcy conjures a small fire as Sophia conjures a wind

that spreads it through the forest. Trees alight on fire as we run through. The flames spread sporadically as Deatra screams in the distance.

Lindy and Clark attempt to use Water to contain the flames, smoke arising from the distinguished fire. We're unable to see properly as the smoke surrounds us.

"We need to fight." Aurelia shouts.

Instead of running away from the battle, we turn back and run towards it. I spot a helicopter and place Jenna in there, Maxine volunteers to stay with her and wishes us luck. Amara and Oscar run forwards and bring two trees down to block the way to the helicopter.

We return to the Dormiton Building, myself and Warren hide behind a wall while everyone else fights. I can see buildings crumbling down as subordinates and Uprisers with the Earth element tear the ground apart and battle. I see Matt Rochon leap to the ground as he falls between a gap.

I see Uprising volunteers and subordinates dropping dead everywhere, I spot Sophia, Alice and Lindy fighting a crowd of subordinates in the far distance.

"Isaac, come on!" Warren shouts as we race into the Dormiton Building, Warren places his hands on the wall causing the building to shake. A subordinate shoots a flame at me as I counter with Water, mist filling the corridor as I shoot again, pummelling the subordinate to the ground.

We race downstairs and into the vaults as Diego comes up behind us. He conjures a jet of water and aims it towards us as flames encroach his body. Darcy emerges behind him. She stops, realising it was her own brother.

"*No.*" She screams.

"We need to end this." I shout. "*Help me.*"

I struggle to open the safe containing the Elementarium Stone when Warren asks me what the numbers on the walls of the control room where when I was stuck in the glass box in the Dormiton.

"I can't *bloody* remember." I snap.

"Try!"

A large group of subordinates rush into the vault as we begin to duel. I project Water onto the staircase and Warren crumbles the ground and Darcy shoots flames onto it. The subordinates slip around as they fight us. Delaney runs in and burns a subordinate as they light her in flames. I don't notice until it's too late, her burnt body lying on the floor amongst the bodies of subordinates and the conjunction of mud that the three of us have created by combining our elements.

I remember.

    Air-71, Earth-39, Fire-02, Water-48.

I frantically type the numbers in as Darcy and Warren fight an ever-growing amount of subordinates. The door opens and a box containing the stone presents itself, Darcy and Warren become overwhelmed with how many subordinates there are as I propel a heavy jet of Water, throwing them all back against the wall as they land on-top of Delaney's body.

We rush outside as the Dormiton Building begins to fall to pieces, racing up to Deatra. She waves her hand and we fly backwards. As I lie on the ground, I see the bodies of volunteers splattered amongst me. Emma Kempton, Alex Nielsen, Ellen Riverson, Kathryn Burris, *all* dead. I hear a scream coming from Maxine as Amara rushes up to me and drags me to the helicopter. Aurelia and Henry fight, Water against Air, as Jenna stirs awake.

"Stop!" She yells, noticing her two parents duelling. "Dad!"

Henry projects a gust of wind that throws Jenna

against the helicopter head first, her body slamming against the floor, everything turning silent as my heart tears into two.

I race to Jenna's body, pleading for to stay with me as Aurelia gets closer to Henry, the two of them crumbling to the ground, distraught in their strident cries as the battle stops. I cradle Jenna in my arms as she looks up at me as Henry hastily runs away.

"Thank you, Isaac, for showing me how to love." She whispers breathlessly as the life in her eyes fade. I close them and bury my head on her shoulder, my cries being muffled.

Aurelia collapses as Robbie emerges from the battle, his arm is so heavily burnt that his flesh seeps through his uniform.

"We're losing." Robbie moans. "She's *too* strong."

"We need to fight. No more avoiding all of this."

As Aurelia and Maxine sit by Jenna's body, the rest of us run into the fight. Streams of Water shoot past us as flames soar above, the ground trembles as the wind howls aggressively, making us unsteady.

Deatra conjures a purple ball of light as Sophia, Alice and Lindy re-join us, looking fairly wounded. Alice shoots a flame towards Deatra as she retaliates, throwing the ball of light towards Alice. Alice takes a step back, screaming in agony as Sophia pushes a gust of wind to Deatra, causing her to fall to the ground. Lindy conjures a spinning sphere of Water and aims it towards Deatra as Alice combines with Lindy by conjuring a ball of Fire that clashes with Water to create a mist that surrounds Deatra. Deatra throws her hands to the side as the mist separates, spinning her right hand in the air as we attempt to fight her. Sophia, Alice and Lindy begin to levitate in the air as Deatra pushes her hand forwards as a portal to the threshold appears.

"Say goodbye, Isaac." She laughs as she blocks Darcy's flames with a purple, force-field-like entity.

"Don't you dare." I shout.

Deatra pushes the three of them into the portal as it closes, then running over the bodies of subordinates and volunteers as we chase her, instead trying to run through the bodies instead of crushing them like Deatra does. We use our elements to try and stop her but she begins to ascend using Aether.

"The throne is mine." Deatra screeches as we begin to combat more subordinates.

A gust of wind pushes me back as a subordinate raises his hand as the ground begins to split. Deatra flies into the Council Building as I jump over the split, thrashing a jet of Water towards the subordinate, pulling my hand back as the Water pulls him back. I raise my hand, the subordinate engulfed in a stream of Water, quickly dropping my hand as the subordinate falls into the abyss.

Amara and Robbie combine elements and create a

stream of ice that flows through the ground, causing subordinates to fall. Robbie pulls his hand back as the subordinates fall forwards and into the abyss. Warren slams his hands onto the ground as the crack closes, trapping the subordinates underneath. He points his left hand at a building as it collapses onto where the crack was as we sprint away.

Clark rushes from the helicopter with the box containing the Clusters.

"Go and get her."

Myself, Robbie, Darcy and Warren run forwards to the Council Building Deatra flew into as Aurelia and Clark fight the few remaining subordinates. Just four battle-torn volunteers remain, perched near Maxine by the helicopter as they recuperate. Henry is stood by the door as we enter the building, pushing his fist upwards as we're thrown to the side. Warren brings down the ceiling above him as Henry leaps out the door, only to be met by Aurelia.

"I forgive you, Henry, I do. I forgive you, because this isn't you, this is Deatra. But, I *cannot* love you anymore. You have stolen love from me. You have taken my child from me and I *hate* you for it." Aurelia cries as she propels a jet of Water onto Henry, thrashing him against the building as blood flows from his head.

We run up the stairs, hearing Deatra laugh from above. Instead of pulling the stairs above us down, Warren aims his hand to the right as the staircase slams into the building as Deatra topples to the ground. Robbie pulls his arm backwards as she falls down to our feet, grabbing hold of my leg as I fight to get her off. I kick around as she pulls me down the stairs, Deatra uses Aether to rebound on the floor as we whip onto a wall. I press my hands on Deatra's head as Water starts wrapping around her head. Robbie creates a barrier of Air that bounds us together as Clark places the Clusters onto Deatra's hands. She screams as I crawl onto the ground, my head pounding from the impact.

"If you do this, you're *just* as bad as me." Deatra mutters, her voice breathless and desperate.

"Nobody could be as bad as you." I yell.

"Subordinates, come out." Deatra yells as Clark drags her to a post and ties her to it, subordinates emerge from a building and charge towards us.

The remaining volunteers, Amara, Oscar and Maxine rush up to us to help fight as I pull the Elementarium Stone out of my pocket. Darcy, Warren, Robbie and I move away as the others protect us. One by one we make a small cut on our hands and drip our blood onto the stone. Veins writhe through our bodies, popping as they turn black. This is the Nether.

"*Unleash her.*" I shout as Clark releases Deatra.

She conjures a strobe of light that she whips towards us as Robbie throws his fist in the air as lightning strikes. I whisk my hand in a circular motion as storm clouds emerge, rain thrashing against us. Warren puts his arms in front of him, clenching his hands as the ground trembles. Darcy emits fireballs and writhing flames as we duel Deatra.

Deatra screams as heavy purple veins pop through her body. She lifts her arms in the air as Robbie strikes her with lightning, my arms grow heavy as I conjure a ball of Water and throw it to Deatra, the rain pattering against us. Warren aims to an upcoming group of subordinates and pushes his fist forward as the ground beneath them drops, causing them to fall. Maxine, Aurelia, Clark and the volunteers continue to fight subordinates with Amara and Oscar as the four of us stand in a line, a dark energy flows from us as it reaches Deatra, her body floating up in the air. She screams as her eyes darken, turning into a coarse black. She struggles to detain the Nether as purple entities fly towards us, one piercing through my shoulder as I drop down.

Deatra screeches in agony as she plummets to the ground, her body is lifeless as I rest against the ground in exhaustion. The subordinates stop fighting as they stand there, shaking, in confusion.

"What's happening?" One asks as Aurelia holds back her element, Maxine and Clark stand in bewilderment.

"Where are we?" Another asks, gripping onto her elbow which looks dislocated.

"It's okay." Aurelia sighs. "It's over."

We make our way back to the helicopter, leaving Deatra's body amongst the bodies of subordinates and volunteers. I cling onto my shoulder as a volunteer tends to Robbie's flesh wound. Warren assists Darcy as she limps onto the helicopter. Aurelia brings out a stretcher and places Jenna onto it, covering her with a white sheet.

"We can give her a proper send-off." Aurelia tells us as Clark assists Aurelia and Jenna's body into a separate helicopter.

Despite arriving with four helicopters, we only need

two to get back to the Uprising Quarter. As the helicopter takes off, I look back at the bodies lying lifeless on the ground, spotting Deatra in her white suit by the edge, sprawled on the ground like everyone else.

"Seems she was human after all." A volunteer remarks.

"You're Jordan, right? Jordan Close?" I ask, Jordan wears the same uniform as us all, with an Air symbol on their shoulder.

"Yes."

"Thank you." I shake Jordan's hand. "Thank *you* for helping."

I lean back, looking out the window as we fly back to the Uprising Quarter. The journey back seems much slower, I sit with Robbie as Darcy and Warren huddle up together. Amara sleeps on Oscar's shoulder as Maxine sits with Clark.

We land at the Uprising Quarter. The Reformation Building is burnt to the core, only the skeleton remaining. We're greeted by a crowd of Uprising Quarter inhabitants, Ange stood at the front as she rushes up to me and hugs me.

"I was *so* worried."

"How did you cope here? Any casualties?" I ask.

"One or two, the subordinates got the short end of the stick." Ange sighs. "I wasn't having it, *not* today. How about you? Any casualties?"

"Delaney and Jenna, a few volunteers too." Darcy tells Ange. "Deatra's gone, though."

"Oh, I'm so sorry." Ange says as she hugs me again. "I know you really liked Jenna."

"I loved her."

Aurelia takes Jenna's body out of the helicopter and into the Elemental Centre, which is barely damaged apart from a hole caused by the helicopter smashing into the windows.

"Hang on, where are Sophia, Alice and Lindy? I don't see them." Ange asks as she looks around.

"We don't know. Deatra's abilities seemed strange, she conjured some kind of portal that threw them into the threshold. They're *gone*, I guess."

"I see; I guess we might see them again someday."

"The Reformation Building, what are we going to do?" Clark asks Ange.

"The underground area's perfectly fine. I guess we'll just rebuild the ground floor area." Ange says as she goes off with Clark, seeming much more talkative than the last time I saw her.

"Your Mother would be proud." Maxine tells Amara

and I. "Your Father and Claude too."

"Thanks, Grandma." Amara hugs her.

"Oh, don't call me that. It makes me feel old, I just *fought* in a battle, just call me Maxine!" She laughs.

I go up to Darcy and Warren and give them both a hug.

"You did good." Warren says.

"You were both great." I tell them.

Warren's family run up to them, their clothes covered in dirt. His brother, Charlie, has a wound on his forehead. They talk as Robbie spots Louis in the crowd, he runs up to him and they embrace as Louis sobs with relief. I smile as I spot Jenna in the distance, walking down to the memorial fountain. She fades away as a tear trails down my cheek. Jordan, the volunteer, comes up to me and says goodbye. The crowd disperses, leaving us alone in the street as the helicopter flies away. Maxine, Amara, Oscar and Clark walk away as Robbie says goodbye to Louis and rejoins us.

Warren comes up from behind and jokingly wraps his arms around me as Darcy laughs, taking hold of Robbie's hand as we walk towards our house. Our clothes are torn but I do not care.

We arrive at the front door to find a box by the side, Warren picks it up and opens it. Inside is a key to the house next door where Sophia, Alice and Lindy lived. Warren puts the key into his pocket as I open the front door to our house, we go into the kitchen and sit around the table. Warren looks lovingly at Darcy as she exhales, I take a deep breath and smile, knowing that despite all this grief I feel, I'm here with my friends and I feel more alive than I've ever felt before.

I'm grateful, and I feel like I can finally live my life.

Epilogue

It's been a week since the 'battle', and a few days since Jenna's funeral. Darcy gave a moving eulogy, and that evening we added Jenna, Delaney, and the others to the memorial fountain.

We've *yet* to find Sophia and Alice, but apparently Lindy was spotted in the South-Western Quarter. Warren used the key that was left on our doorstep to get into their house, he went in and found a bouquet of white roses left on their kitchen table.

I walk down to the Elemental Centre with Warren, and we're greeted by Robbie and Louis who have reconciled. Ange has already begun rebuilding the Reformation Building with Clark's assistance, so we can hear construction work as we knock on the door to Maxine's temporary office.

Maxine has become a councillor here, Aurelia's on leave for obvious reasons.

"Ah, boys, come in." Maxine says.

"What's the news?" Robbie asks.

"Good news and bad news. We're restricting the use of the elements to army-use only." Maxine informs us.

"Is that the good news?" I ask, approving of this.

"Well, we want to offer *you* important roles in the New Elemental Army."

Robbie and Louis sign up instantly, however both Warren and I look at each other, smirk, then politely decline.

"No thanks." We say in unison, walking out of the Elemental Centre and to the memorial fountain.

"Was that the right choice to make?" Warren asks me.

"What's this?" Darcy asks as she comes up behind us.

"We just declined roles in the New Elemental Army." Warren tells her as they greet each other with a kiss.

"Why?" She asks us.

"I don't know, just a bit tired of fighting I guess." I tell her, to which Warren agrees by nodding his head.

"Fair enough, Maxine asked me earlier and I declined as well." Darcy laughs as she skims her fingers over the engraved names of those we lost.

The three of us walk towards the Reformation Building as Warren wraps his arms around the both of us.

"*Come quick.*" Robbie shouts.

We run back into the Elemental Centre and into the office.

"Hello? Can anyone help me?" A voice says from Maxine's computer; she turns the screen around to show a video of Arthur Allstrong tied to a chair.

"Arthur Allstrong? He's *alive*?" I ask.

"Hello?" The voice calls out.

ABOUT THE AUTHOR

Curtis Smith is a blogger for Totally Culture with a passion for media production and entertainment. Born in Guildford to a deaf family, he was taught how to use British Sign Language from a young age and has continued to embrace the deaf community. Aside from using his blog to talk about feminism, pop culture and diversity in the media industry, Curtis can also be found binge-watching various sci-fi or comedy television programmes as well as trying to organise flash mobs, which has only truly been successful once.

Having started The Rising of the Elements back in 2012, Curtis took a break in 2014 and returned to writing in 2015 after completing his A-Level studies in the same year, then completing the novel in 2016 during his gap year.

Printed in Great Britain
by Amazon